In the poignantly beautiful, powerful LAST SEPTEMBER, Margaret Turner is finally reunited with Susan Lathrop, the childhood playmate who has haunted her thoughts in bittersweet memory. The two women confront their own lives as well as each other — and under the most dramatic of circumstances: within "the extraordinary, sweet, concentrated air which runs under the great dark wings of a hurricane."

Said the *New York Times* of *LAST SEPTEMBER:* "It *...places Miss Hull in the company of novelists like Edith Wharton and Willa Cather.* ... *[It] will live as a classic, equal in stature to Ethan Fromme* and *The Red Badge of Courage.* ... Its quality may be compared to *Death Comes to the Archbishop.*"

In eighty-three years of life, much of it spent with Mabel Louise Robinson, Helen R. Hull produced seventeen novels, four works on the craft of writing, and sixty-five short stories. This special edition of LAST SEPTEMBER celebrates one of our finest writers — on the one hundredth anniversary of her birth.

LAST SEPTEMBER

by
Helen R. Hull

NAIAD
1988

Printed in the United States of America
First Edition

Cover design by The Women's Graphic Center
Typesetting by Sandi Stancil

The stories in this collection, and the novella, Last September, first appeared in magazines as follows: The Fire (*Century* 95 November, 1917); Alley Ways (*Century* 95 February, 1918); Separation (*Touchstone* 6 March, 1920); Groping (*Seven Arts* 1 February, 1917); Discovery (*Touchstone* 3 August, 1918); The Fusing (*Touchstone* 5 July, 1919); Last September (*Good Housekeeping* 109 (July, 1939).

The pictures of Helen R. Hull and Mabel L. Robinson used in this book are the property of Columbia University and are used with the kind permission to reproduce them from the Rare Book and Manuscript Library, Columbia University.

The illustration on page 52 is the original illustration for the short story, "Alley Ways," as it appeared in Century Magazine, February, 1918.

ISBN 0-941483-09-6

About the Author

Pat Miller, like Helen Hull, grew up in the Midwest and transplanted herself to the east coast, where for many years she taught in the Women's Studies Program at the University of Connecticut. Recently she organized her own consulting business as an editor and writer: The Well-Tempered Sentence. She is currently working on reprinting several of Hull's novels and writing a biography of Hull and Mabel Louise Robinson — a process that she says resembles living in her very own detective novel.

For Helen R. Hull and Mabel L. Robinson

*After all the years you dedicated your books
to each other, here at last is one in honor
of your life together.*

Contents

Introduction . . . . *xi*

The Fire 1

Separation 19

Alley Ways 31

Groping 53

Discovery 75

The Fusing 93

Last September 113

Afterword 181

Illustrations 52, 74, 92, 112, 180

Introduction

On their way from Maine to New York in September 1938, Helen Hull and her life's companion Mabel Louise Robinson drove straight into the Hurricane of 1938, finding shelter in Providence, Rhode Island, at the last moment — just before their car was submerged and, along with it, typewriters, suitcases, and much of their summer's writing. Their close brush with the devastation of the 1938 storm became a seed for "Last September," the dramatic title story of this collection.

We know even less about the other, earlier stories in this volume, all of which were published between 1917 and 1921 in *Century, Seven Arts,* and *Touchstone* magazines. In fact, we know only one thing for certain: just as Hull "sat down to work on Cynthia" one summer morning in 1917, the plaster ceiling collapsed, fortunately not on her. So much for the rich, personal detail of literary history.

"Last September" first appeared in July 1939 in *Good Housekeeping.* When it was re-issued in Hull's book *Experiment* in 1940, the *New York Times* reviewer swore that the story would become a classic, equal in literary fame to *Ethan Frome* and *The Red Badge of Courage.* At the time, Hull was a prolific and respected writer. Her publisher and friend, Thomas R. Coward, however, once wrote to her that her situation was much like Ellen Glasgow's: "the books you write [chiefly about family life] and the kind of life you lead, are not particularly suited to publicity stunts." In fact, when interviewers ventured questions about her personal life, Hull was obliged to trot out her wire-haired terrier as proof that the milk of human kindness flowed in her unmarried veins. Hull died in 1971, greatly disappointed that her work had faded so fast from view.

The oldest of four children, Helen Rose Hull was born in Albion, Michigan, on March 28, 1888. She taught school for several years before finishing a Ph.B. at the University of Chicago. In the fall of 1912, she was hired as an instructor in the English Department at Wellesley College in Massachusetts, whereupon she happily transplanted herself to the east coast for the rest of her life.

It was at Wellesley, in the days of women's struggle for the right to vote, that her budding political consciousness began to flower; it continued to blossom in

New York City, where, in 1915, she joined the feminist club Heterodoxy and marched in suffrage parades. But it was at Wellesley, in its community of lively, independent women, many of them living in "Wellesley marriages" with each other, that she met Mabel Louise Robinson. In 1914, Hull and Robinson spent the summer together in Maine, the beginning of a pattern which was to persist until Robinson was too ill to travel from New York in the late 1950s. In Maine, along with several other households of women, they spent their summers writing. It was an arrangement that enabled Helen Hull to publish 17 novels, four books about writing, and some 65 short stories, despite a full-time job at Columbia University, where both she and Robinson taught creative writing for over 40 years.

In "Last September," Margaret Turner and Susan Lathrop come full circle in their lives, returning to each other at the end of their days. The publication of this volume of stories is also a return of sorts: a coming back to the work of Helen Hull. This collection of a few of her many stories commemorates the one hundredth anniversary of her birth; it is published in the hope that a new generation of readers will begin to know her work and to appreciate her life.

In the preparation of this volume, I gratefully acknowledge the assistance of Frederick and Eileen Hull; Judith Schwarz; the Alternative Press Collection, the University of Connecticut; the Rare Book and Manuscript Library, Columbia University; Joan Joffe Hall; William Curtin; and, always, Barbara Drygulski Wright.

Patricia McClelland Miller
Ashford, Connecticut

THE FIRE

Cynthia blotted the entry in the old ledger and scowled across the empty office at the door. Mrs. Moriety had left it ajar when she departed with her receipt for the weekly fifty cents on her "lot." If you supplied the missing gilt letters, you could read the sign on the glass of the upper half: "H. P. Bates. Real Estate. Notary Public." Through the door at Cynthia's elbow came the rumbling voice of old Fleming, the lawyer down the hall; he had come in for his Saturday night game of chess with her father.

1

Cynthia pushed the ledger away from her, and with her elbows on the spotted, green felt of the desk, her fingers burrowing into her cheeks, waited for two minutes by the nickel clock; then, with a quick, awkward movement, she pushed back her chair and plunged to the doorway, her young face twisted in a sort of fluttering resolution.

"Father —"

Her father jerked his head toward her, his fingers poised over a pawn. Old Fleming did not look up.

"Father, I don't think anybody else will be in."

"Well, go on home, then." Her father bent again over the squares, the light shining strongly on the thin places about his temples.

"Father, please," — Cynthia spoke hurriedly, — "you aren't going for a while? I want to go down to Miss Egert's for a minute."

"Eh? What's that?" He leaned back in his chair now, and Mr. Fleming lifted his severe, black beard to look at this intruder. "What for? You can't take any more painting lessons. Your mother doesn't want you going there any more."

"I just want to get some things I left there. I can get back to go home with you."

"But your mother said she didn't like your hanging around down there in an empty house with an old maid. What did she tell you about it?"

"Couldn't I just get my sketches, Father, and tell Miss Egert I'm not coming any more? She would think it was awfully funny if I didn't. I won't stay. But she — she's been good to me —"

"What set your mother against her, then? What you been doing down there?"

Cynthia twisted her hands together, her eyes running from Fleming's amused stare to her father's indecision. Only an accumulated determination could have carried her on into speech. "I've just gone down once a week for a lesson. I want to get my things. If I'm not going, I ought to tell her."

"Why didn't you tell her that last week?"

"I kept hoping I could go on."

"Um." Her father's glance wavered toward his game. "Isn't it too late?"

"Just eight, Father." She stepped near her father, color flooding her cheeks. "If you'll give me ten cents, I can take the car —"

"Well —" He dug into his pocket, nodding at Fleming's grunt, "The women always want cash, eh, Bates?"

Then Cynthia, the dime pressed into her palm, tiptoed across to the nail where her hat and sweater hung, seized them, and still on tiptoe, lest she disturb the game again, ran out to the head of the stairs.

She was trembling as she pulled on her sweater; as she ran down the dark steps to the street the tremble changed to a quiver of excitement. Suppose her father had known just what her mother *had* said! That she could not see Miss Egert again; could never go hurrying down to the cluttered room they called the studio for more of those strange hours of eagerness and pain when she bent over the drawing-board, struggling with the mysteries of color. That last sketch — the little, purpling mint-leaves from the garden — Miss Egert had liked that. And they thought she could leave those sketches there! Leave Miss Egert, too, wondering why she never came again! She hurried to the corner, past the bright store-windows. In thought she could see Miss Egert setting out the jar of

3

brushes, the dishes of water, pushing back the litter of magazines and books to make room for the drawing-board, waiting for her to come. Oh, she had to go once more, black as her disobedience was!

The half-past-eight car was just swinging round the curve. She settled herself behind two German housewives, shawls over their heads, market-baskets beside them. They lived out at the end of the street; one of them sometimes came to the office with payments on her son's lot. Cynthia pressed against the dirty window, fearful lest she miss the corner. There it was, the new street light shining on the sedate old house! She ran to the platform, pushing against the arm the conductor extended.

"Wait a minute, there!" He released her as the car stopped, and she fled across the street.

In front of the house she could not see a light, up-stairs or down, except staring reflections in the windows from the white arc light. She walked past the dark line of box which led to the front door. At the side of the old square dwelling jutted a new, low wing; and there in two windows were soft slits of light along the curtain-edges. Cynthia walked along a little dirt path to a door at the side of the wing. Standing on the door-step, she felt in the shadow for a knocker. As she let it fall, from the garden behind her came a voice:

"I'm out here. Who is it?" There was a noise of feet hurrying through dead leaves, and as Cynthia turned to answer, out of the shadow moved a blur of face and white blouse.

"Cynthia! How nice!" The woman touched Cynthia's shoulder as she pushed open the door. "There, come in."

The candles on the table bent their flames in the draft; Cynthia followed Miss Egert into the room.

4

"You're busy?" Miss Egert had stood up by the door an old wooden-toothed rake. "I don't want to bother you." Cynthia's solemn, young eyes implored the woman and turned hastily away. The intensity of defiance which had brought her at such an hour left her confused.

"Bother? I was afraid I had to have my grand bonfire alone. Now we can have it a party. You'd like to?"

Miss Egert darted across to straighten one of the candles. The light caught in the folds of her crumpled blouse, in the soft, drab hair blown out around her face.

"I can't stay very long." Cynthia stared about the room, struggling to hide her turmoil under ordinary casualness. "You had the carpenter fix the bookshelves, didn't you?"

"Isn't it nice now! All white and gray and restful — just a spark of life in that mad rug. A good place to sit in and grow old."

Cynthia looked at the rug, a bit of scarlet Indian weaving. She wouldn't see it again! The thought poked a derisive finger into her heart.

"Shall we sit down just a minute and then go have the fire?"

Cynthia dropped into the wicker chair, wrenching her fingers through one another.

"My brother came in to-night, his last attempt to make me see reason," said Miss Egert.

Cynthia lifted her eyes. Miss Egert wasn't wondering why she had come; she could stay without trying to explain.

Miss Egert wound her arms about her knees as she went on talking. Her slight body was wrenched a little out of symmetry, as though from straining always for something uncaptured; there was the same lack of symmetry in her face, in her eyebrows, in the line of her

5

mobile lips. But her eyes had nothing fugitive, nothing pursuing in their soft, gray depth. Their warm, steady eagerness shone out in her voice, too, in its swift inflections.

"I tried to show him it wasn't a bit disgraceful for me to live here in a wing of my own instead of being a sort of nurse-maid adjunct in his house." She laughed, a soft, throaty sound. "It's my house. It's all I have left to keep me a person, you see. I won't get out and be respectable in his eyes."

"He didn't mind your staying here and taking care of — them!" cried Cynthia.

"It's respectable, dear, for an old maid to care for her father and mother; but when they die she ought to be useful to some one else instead of renting her house and living on an edge of it."

"Oh," — Cynthia leaned forward, — "I should think you'd hate him! I think families are — terrible!"

"Hate him?" Miss Egert smiled. "He's nice. He just doesn't agree with me. As long as he lets the children come over — I told him I meant to have a beautiful time with them, with my real friends — with you."

Cynthia shrank into her chair, her eyes tragic again.

"Come, let's have our bonfire!" Miss Egert, with a quick movement, stood in front of Cynthia, one hand extended.

Cynthia crouched away from the hand.

"Miss Egert," — her voice came out in a desperate little gasp, — "I can't come down any more. I can't take any more painting lessons." She stopped. Miss Egert waited, her head tipped to one side. "Mother doesn't think I better. I came down — after my things."

"They're all in the workroom." Miss Egert spoke quietly. "Do you want them now?"

"Yes." Cynthia pressed her knuckles against her lips. Over her hand her eyes cried out. "Yes, I better get them," she said heavily.

Miss Egert, turning slowly, lifted a candle from the table. "We'll have to take this. The wiring isn't done." She crossed the room, her thin fingers, not quite steady, bending around the flame.

Cynthia followed through a narrow passage. Miss Egert pushed open a door, and the musty odor of the store-room floated out into a queer chord with the fresh plaster of the hall.

"Be careful of that box!" Miss Egert set the candle on a pile of trunks. "I've had to move all the truck from the attic and studio in here. Your sketches are in the portfolio, and that's — somewhere!"

Cynthia stood in the doorway, watching Miss Egert bend over a pile of canvases, throwing up a grotesque, rounded shadow on the wall. Round the girl's throat closed a ring of iron.

"Here they are, piled up —"

Cynthia edged between the boxes. Miss Egert was dragging the black portfolio from beneath a pile of books.

"And here's the book I wanted you to see." The pile slipped crashing to the floor as Miss Egert pulled out a magazine. "Never mind those. See here." She dropped into the chair from which she had knocked the books, the portfolio under one arm, the free hand running through the pages of an old art magazine. The chair swung slightly; Cynthia, peering down between the boxes, gave a startled "Oh!"

"What is it?" Miss Egert followed Cynthia's finger. "The chair?" She was silent a moment. "Do you think I keep my mother prisoner here in a wheel-chair now that

7

she is free?" She ran her hand along the worn arm. "I tried to give it to an old ladies' home, but it was too used up. They wanted more style."

"But doesn't it remind you —" Cynthia hesitated.

"It isn't fair to remember the years she had to sit here waiting to die. You didn't know her. I've been going back to the real years —" Miss Egert smiled at Cynthia's bewildered eyes. "Here, let's look at these." She turned another page. "See, Cynthia. Aren't they swift and glad? That's what I was trying to tell you the other day. See that arm, and the drapery there! Just a line —" The girl bent over the page, frowning at the details the quick finger pointed out. "Don't they catch you along with them?" She held the book out at arm's-length, squinting at the figures. "Take it along. There are several more." She tucked the book into the portfolio and rose. "Come on; we'll have our fire."

"But, Miss Egert," — Cynthia's voice hardened as she was swept back into her own misery, — "I can't take it. I can't come any more."

"To return a book?" Miss Egert lowered her eyelids as if she were again sizing up a composition. "You needn't come just for lessons."

Cynthia shook her head.

"Mother thinks —" She fell into silence. She couldn't say what her mother thought — dreadful things. If she could only swallow the hot pressure in her throat!

"Oh. I hadn't understood." Miss Egert's fingers paused for a swift touch on Cynthia's arm, and then reached for the candle. "You can go on working by yourself."

"It isn't that —" Cynthia struggled an instant, and dropped into silence again. She couldn't say out loud any of the things she was feeling. There were too many walls

8

between feeling and speech: loyalty to her mother, embarrassment that feelings should come so near words, a fear of hurting Miss Egert. "Don't mind so much, Cynthia." Miss Egert led the way back to the living-room. "You can stay for the bonfire? That will be better than sitting here. Run into the kitchen and bring the matches and marshmallows — in a dish in the cupboard."

Cynthia, in the doorway, stared at Miss Egert. Didn't she care at all! Then the dumb ache in her throat stopped throbbing as Miss Egert's gray eyes held her steadily a moment. She did care! She did! She was just helping her. Cynthia took the candle and went back through the passageway to the kitchen, down at the very end.

She made a place on the table in the litter of dishes and milk-bottles for the candle. The matches had been spilled on the shelf of the stove and into the sink. Cynthia gathered a handful of the driest. Shiftlessness was one of her mother's counts against Miss Egert. Cynthia flushed as she recalled her stumbling defense: Miss Egert had more important things to do; dishes were kept in their proper place; and her mother's: "Important! Mooning about!"

"Find them, Cynthia?" The clear, low voice came down the hall, and Cynthia hurried back.

Out in the garden it was quite black. As they came to the far end, the old stone wall made a dark bank against the sky, with a sharp star over its edge. Miss Egert knelt; almost with the scratch of the match the garden leaped into yellow, with fantastic moving shadows from the trees and in the corner of the wall. She raked leaves over the blaze, pulled the great mound into firmer shape, and then drew Cynthia back under the wall to watch. The light ran over her face; the delighted gestures of her hands were like quick shadows.

"See the old apple-tree dance! He's too old to move fast."

Cynthia crouched by the wall, brushing away from her face the scratchy leaves of the dead hollyhocks. Excitement tingled through her; she felt the red and yellow flames seizing her, burning out the heavy rebellion, the choking weight. Miss Egert leaned back against the wall, her hands spread so that her thin fingers were fire-edged.

"See the smoke curl up through those branches! Isn't it lovely, Cynthia?" She darted around the pile to push more leaves into the flames.

Cynthia strained forward, hugging her arms to her body. Never had there been such a fire! It burned through her awkwardness, her self-consciousness. It ate into the thick, murky veils which hung always between her and the things she struggled to find out. She took a long breath, and the crisp scent of smoke from the dead leaves tingled down through her body.

Miss Egert was at her side again. Cynthia looked up; the slight, asymmetrical figure was like the apple-tree, still, yet dancing!

"Why don't you paint it?" demanded Cynthia, abruptly, and then was frightened as Miss Egert's body stiffened, lost its suggestion of motion.

"I can't." The woman dropped to the ground beside Cynthia, crumpling a handful of leaves. "It's too late." She looked straight at the fire. "I must be content to see it." She blew the pieces of leaves from the palm of her hand and smiled at Cynthia. "Perhaps some day you'll paint it — or write it."

10

"I can't paint." Cynthia's voice quivered. "I want to do something. I can't even see things except what you point out. And now —"

Miss Egert laid one hand over Cynthia's clenched fingers. The girl trembled at the cold touch. "You must go on looking." The glow, as the flames died lower, flushed her face. "Cynthia, you're just beginning. You mustn't stop just because you aren't to come here any more. I don't know whether you can say things with your brush; but you must find them out. You mustn't shut your eyes again."

"It's hard alone."

"That doesn't matter."

Cynthia's fingers unclasped, and one hand closed desperately around Miss Egert's. Her heart fluttered in her temples, her throat, her breast. She clung to the fingers, pulling herself slowly up from an inarticulate abyss.

"Miss Egert," — she stumbled into words, — "I can't bear it, not coming here! Nobody else cares except about sensible things. You do, beautiful, wonderful things."

"You'd have to find them for yourself, Cynthia." Miss Egert's fingers moved under the girl's grasp. Then she bent toward Cynthia, and kissed her with soft, pale lips that trembled against the girl's mouth. "Cynthia, don't let any one stop you! Keep searching!" She drew back, poised for a moment in the shadow before she rose. Through Cynthia ran the swift feet of white ecstasy. She was pledging herself to some tremendous mystery, which trembled all about her.

"Come, Cynthia, we're wasting our coals."

Miss Egert held out her hands. Cynthia, laying hers in them, was drawn to her feet. As she stood there, inarticulate, full of a strange, excited, shouting hope,

11

behind them the path crunched. Miss Egert turned, and Cynthia shrank back.

Her mother stood in the path, making no response to Miss Egert's "Good evening, Mrs. Bates."

The fire had burned too low to lift the shadow from the mother's face. Cynthia could see the hem of her skirt swaying where it dipped up in front. Above that two rigid hands in gray cotton gloves; above that the suggestion of a white, strained face.

Cynthia took a little step toward her.

"I came to get my sketches," she implored her. Her throat was dry. What if her mother began to say cruel things — the things she had already said at home.

"I hope I haven't kept Cynthia too late," Miss Egert said. "We were going to toast marshmallows. Won't you have one, Mrs. Bates?" She pushed the glowing leaf-ashes together. The little spurt of flame showed Cynthia her mother's eyes; hard, angry, resting an instant on Miss Egert and then assailing her.

"Cynthia knows she should not be here. She is not permitted to run about the streets alone at night."

"Oh, I'm sorry." Miss Egert made a deprecating little gesture. "But no harm has come to her."

"She has disobeyed me."

At the tone of her mother's voice Cynthia felt something within her breast curl up like a leaf caught in flame.

"I'll get the things I came for." She started toward the house, running past her mother. She must hurry, before her mother said anything to hurt Miss Egert.

She stumbled on the door-step, and flung herself against the door. The portfolio was across the room, on the little, old piano. The candle beside it had guttered down over the cover. Cynthia pressed out the wobbly

12

flame, and, hugging the portfolio, ran back across the room. On the threshold she turned for a last glimpse. The row of Botticelli details over the bookcases were blurred into gray in the light of the one remaining candle; the Indian rug had a wavering glow. Then she heard Miss Egert just outside.

"I'm sorry Cynthia isn't to come any more," she was saying.

Cynthia stepped forward. The two women stood in the dim light, her mother's thickened, settled body stiff and hostile, Miss Egert's slight figure swaying toward her gently.

"Cynthia has a good deal to do," her mother answered. "We can't afford to give her painting lessons, especially —" Cynthia moved down between the women — "especially," her mother continued, "as she doesn't seem to get much of anywhere. You'd think she'd have some pictures to show after so many lessons."

"Perhaps I'm not a good teacher. Of course she's just beginning."

"She'd better put her time on her studies."

"I'll miss her. We've had some pleasant times together."

Cynthia held out her hand toward Miss Egert, with a fearful little glance at her mother.

"Good-by, Miss Egert."

Miss Egert's cold fingers pressed it an instant.

"Good night, Cynthia," she said slowly.

Then Cynthia followed her mother's silent figure along the path; she turned her head as they reached the sidewalk. Back in the garden winked the red eye of the fire.

They waited under the arc light for the car, Cynthia stealing fleeting glances at her mother's averted face. On

13

the car she drooped against the window-edge, away from
her mother's heavy silence. She was frightened now, a
panicky child caught in disobedience. Once, as the car
turned at the corner below her father's office, she spoke:

"Father will expect me —"

"He knows I went after you," was her mother's grim
answer.

Cynthia followed her mother into the house. Her
small brother was in the sitting-room, reading. He looked
up from his book with wide, knowing eyes. Rebellious
humiliation washed over Cynthia; setting her lips against
their quivering, she pulled off her sweater.

"Go on to bed, Robert," called her mother from the
entry, where she was hanging her coat. "You've sat up too
late as it is."

He yawned, and dragged his feet with provoking
slowness past Cynthia.

"Was she down there, Mama?" He stopped on the
bottom step to grin at his sister.

"Go on, Robert. Start your bath. Mother'll be up in a
minute."

"Aw, it's too late for a bath." He leaned over the rail.

"It's Saturday. I couldn't get back sooner."

Cynthia swung away from the round, grinning face.
Her mother went past her into the dining-room. Robert
shuffled upstairs; she heard the water splashing into the
tub.

Her mother was very angry with her. Presently she
would come back, would begin to speak. Cynthia shivered.
The familiar room seemed full of hostile, accusing silence,
like that of her mother. If only she had come straight
home from the office, she would be sitting by the table in
the old Morris chair, reading, with her mother across from
her sewing, or glancing through the evening paper. She

gazed about the room at the neat scrolls of the brown wall-paper, at a picture above the couch, cows by a stream. The dull, ordinary comfort of life there hung about her, a reproaching shadow, within which she felt the heavy, silent discomfort her transgression dragged after it. It would be much easier to go on just as she was expected to do. Easier. The girl straightened her drooping body. That things were hard didn't matter. Miss Egert had insisted upon that. She was forgetting the pledge she had given. The humiliation slipped away, and a cold exaltation trembled through her, a remote echo of the hope that had shouted within her back there in the garden. Here it was difficult to know what she had promised, to what she had pledged herself — something that the familiar, comfortable room had no part in.

She glanced toward the dining-room, and her breath quickened. Between the faded green portières stood her mother, watching her with hard, bright eyes. Cynthia's glance faltered; she looked desperately about the room as if hurrying her thoughts to some shelter. Beside her on the couch lay the portfolio. She took a little step toward it, stopping at her mother's voice.

"Well, Cynthia, have you anything to say?"

Cynthia lifted her eyes.

"Don't you think I have trouble enough with your brothers? You, a grown girl, defying me! I can't understand it."

"I went down for this." Cynthia touched the black case.

"Put that down! I don't want to see it!" The mother's voice rose, breaking down the terrifying silences. "You disobeyed me. I told you you weren't to go there again. And then I telephoned your father to ask you to do an errand for me, and find you there — with that woman!"

15

"I'm not going again." Cynthia twisted her hands together. "I had to go a last time. She was a friend. I could not tell her I wasn't coming —"

"A friend! A sentimental old maid, older than your mother! Is that a friend for a young girl? What were you doing when I found you? Holding hands! Is that the right thing for you? She's turned your head. You aren't the same Cynthia, running off to her, complaining of your mother."

"Oh, no!" Cynthia flung out her hand. "We were just talking." Her misery confused her.

"Talking? About what?"

"About — The recollection rushed through Cynthia — "about beauty." She winced, a flush sweeping up to the edge of her fair hair, at her mother's laugh.

"Beauty! You disobey your mother, hurt her, to talk about beauty at night with an old maid!"

There was a hot beating in Cynthia's throat; she drew back against the couch.

"Pretending to be an artist," her mother drove on, "to get young girls who are foolish enough to listen to her sentimentalizing."

"She was an artist," pleaded Cynthia. "She gave it up to take care of her father and mother. I told you all about that —"

"Talking about beauty doesn't make artists."

Cynthia stared at her mother. She had stepped near the table, and the light through the green shade of the reading-lamp made queer pools of color about her eyes, in the waves of her dark hair. She didn't look real. Cynthia threw one hand up against her lips. She was sucked down and down in an eddy of despair. Her mother's voice dragged her again to the surface.

16

"We let you go there because you wanted to paint, and you maunder and say things you'd be ashamed to have your mother hear. I've spent my life working for you, planning for you, and you go running off —" Her voice broke into a new note, a trembling, grieved tone. "I've always trusted you, depended on you; now I can't even trust you."

"I won't go there again. I had to explain."

"I can't believe you. You don't care how you make me feel."

Cynthia was whirled again down the sides of the eddy.

"I can't believe you care anything for me, your own mother."

Cynthia plucked at the braid on her cuff.

"I didn't do it to make you sorry," she whispered. "I — it was —" The eddy closed about her, and with a little gasp she dropped down on the couch, burying her head in the sharp angle of her elbows.

The mother took another step toward the girl; her hand hovered above the bent head and then dropped.

"You know mother wants just what is best for you, don't you? I can't let you drift away from us, your head full of silly notions."

Cynthia's shoulders jerked. From the head of the stairs came Robert's shout:

"Mama, tub's full!"

"Yes; I'm coming."

Cynthia stood up. She was not crying. About her eyes and nostrils strained the white intensity of hunger.

"You don't think —" She stopped, struggling with her habit of inarticulateness. "There might be things — not silly — you might not see what —"

"Cynthia!" The softness snapped out of the mother's voice.

17

Cynthia stumbled up to her feet; she was as tall as her mother. For an instant they faced each other, and then the mother turned away, her eyes tear-brightened. Cynthia put out an awkward hand.

"Mother," she said piteously, "I'd like to tell you — I'm sorry —"

"You'll have to show me you are by what you do." The woman started wearily up the stairs. "Go to bed. It's late."

Cynthia waited until the bathroom door closed upon Robert's splashings. She climbed the stairs slowly, and shut herself into her room. She laid the portfolio in the bottom drawer of her white bureau; then she stood by her window. Outside, the big elm-tree, in fine, leafless dignity, showed dimly against the sky, a few stars caught in the arch of its branches.

A swift, tearing current of rebellion swept away her unhappiness, her confused misery; they were bits of refuse in this new flood. She saw, with a fierce, young finality that she was pledged to a conflict as well as to a search. As she knelt by the window and pressed her cheek on the cool glass, she felt the house about her, with its pressure of useful, homely things, as a very prison. No more journeyings down to Miss Egert's for glimpses of escape. She must find her own ways. Keep searching! At the phrase, excitement again glowed within her; she saw the last red wink of the fire in the garden.

SEPARATION

"Where are you going, Cynthia?"

"I told you." To the child at the door, the query tugged at a rope that held her. She pulled away, hotly. "You said I might go this afternoon!"

"Are you going over to that Mrs. Moore's again?"

"I've finished practicing. And I haven't been there for a long time. You said —" Her voice quivered. She knew that such words served only to tighten the rope.

"She's a stranger here in town. I don't approve of her encouraging you — putting silly notions in your head. It isn't a good thing. And what does she want with you, a little girl?"

Cynthia held her breath; if she said a word she would, she knew, sound "impertinent."

"What do you do there? You can't sit down at home with your mother, like a nice girl, but you must go tearing over there. She has made you sulky and secretive, too."

"I'll be home early." Tears under Cynthia's lashes now.

"Oh, well, go on." She looked up from her sewing. "But I hope this will be the last time!"

Cynthia pushed open the door and went down the steps into the sunlight, her mother's words following her like an assured little threat. Perhaps they were just a final tug at the rope, to be sure it still held. Cynthia thought, miserably, of her resolve, only last night, to "be good," as her mother put it. Here she was, all awry again! Then warm exultation dried her tears. She had, after all, won out again. The rope was frayed; some day she might break it. She did not think of it as a rope; she felt it as something binding her, holding her back in childhood, tying her away from a strange new self which struggled uncouthly within her.

The cool spring sun threw slanting shadows on the grass and muddy road. Cynthia, hesitating at the corner, had a vague discontent with the street. It looked unkempt, shabby, as though the pricking of green along the edges of the trees, the clear blue of the sky, put to shame the bits of stick and dead leaves in the gutter, the gray poultry yards and sheds behind the houses, the houses themselves, veined with gaunt brown vines. She

20

wondered whether there were violets yet in the woods across the meadow. If she looked, she would be late. But she saw herself, her hands full of violets, climbing the steps of Mrs. Moore's house, and suddenly she was off.

* * * * *

The little side street stopped at the pasture. Cynthia ran across the soft ground, thrilling at the points of fresh green which pushed up through the dead grass. Perhaps it was too early for violets; she couldn't remember when she had found them last year. She crawled between rusty wires of the fence around the wood, and peered about, breathing quickly. Gray-brown leaves thick under her feet, wet black trunks of trees; a faint prickling smell of spring through the old odors of winter. She moved slowly forward, listening to the sound of the leaves under her feet, and then the sound of running water. It was too early; her eagerness sagged. Perhaps, if she could find that brook — Down a little hill she came upon it, a small brook running over dead leaves and stones, yellowed spume marking its spent violence. Suddenly from its edge a bit of purple sang out to her, and Cynthia dropped to her knees beside it. A purple star, poised on its soft stem, with small heavy buds pushing up beside it from a patina of brown-purple leaves. Not a violet, but lovelier!

Cynthia laid a finger on the cool small petals. Then, as she knelt, her face near the ground, she saw not far away the dead matted leaves pried apart, and rising, the buds still curved from their thrust, another hepatica; beyond that another, and then another. If she watched, she might see the whole slope moving, torn apart, by the tender, quiet pressure of the buds. She felt that pressure, as

21

though the buds thrust themselves, blue and purple tipped, up through her body, and she was leaf-mould and hepaticas; no, it was the slope itself that ached and tingled with slow, exquisite pain.

The shriek of a crow swinging over the wood broke the moment, and Cynthia glanced behind her, her face hot. How silly she must look, on her knees in the woods! Suppose Mrs. Moore should see her there — what would she think? She could almost believe she saw her friend, coming down the slope, hear her soft voice, "Why, Cynthia, child! You, here?" Then she could show her the hepaticas — Cynthia's eyes were misty-bright. The crow cawed again, and Cynthia hated him for laughing at her. But she knew Mrs. Moore wouldn't come to the woods. It was too muddy. She pushed the leaves away from the one plant which had blossomed, and digging with her fingers into the soft mould, loosened it, slipped her hand under it, and scrambled up the little hill, back to the street.

The walk through the town was many things. Outwardly, it was the progress of a girl, gawky of elbows and legs, with thin, ungraceful figure, light hair blowing about her face, the black ribbon which tied it flopping at her neck, her head thrust forward, her blue eyes intent. Inwardly, it was a thing of beauty and wonder. A priestess swift of foot climbing the approach to the temple of the goddess she served. A lover, eager to meet his mistress. A brilliant spectacle of shifting scenes, brilliant and yet vague, as though a curtain hung between them and the child, a fear that she might find them suddenly too ridiculous. She threw herself into the path of plunging horses, to rescue this friend; then, dying, she whispered, "It was nothing —" Some tremendous test of love, such as the old knights had endured — "I could not love thee, dear, so much, loved I not honor more!" Cynthia, not Elaine the Lily Maid, on her barge, with the world wondering at the great love of which she had died. Then she had reached the street, had passed the corner, could see the house. None of those things would happen, she knew. She would sit opposite Mrs. Moore, trying clumsily to answer her questions about school, about the people in the town. Perhaps Mrs. Moore would say again that she was glad to see Cynthia, that she was lonely.

* * * * *

Her heart began to beat so quickly that her face felt red to the tip of her nose. She saw with dismay the gray mud caked on her shoes, the black line on her fingers where she had dug into the mould. Slowly she climbed the steps and rang the bell. At its sound, faint within the house, the center of her body contracted — almost, she thought, as if she were very hungry. But she couldn't run; someone was crossing the hall. She saw, back of the ornate "M"" of the lace curtain at the door, a dark head. Then the door opened, and Mrs. Moore was saying, "Oh, it's you, Cynthia!" Her large, prominent eyes seemed blacker, more glittering than usual. "Come in."

Cynthia followed her; she tried to remember the beautiful speech she had made up that morning. It was gone, along with the bright wonder of her walk, and she said, shyly:

"You — you aren't busy — or anything?"

"Just sewing." Mrs. Moore sat down in her wicker rocker by the window. "I'm glad you came in. I was going to send for you."

Cynthia extended her hand, the hepatica drooping in her palm.

"I found it in the woods," she said. "I thought there would be violets, perhaps. But this was out."

"Oh, yes. A pretty little flower." Mrs. Moore squinted at it over the needle she was threading. "Just put it on that paper, Cynthia, so the mud won't get on the table."

Cynthia laid it down. Why had it seemed so lovely in the woods! Awkwardly she seated herself, trying to tuck her muddy shoes under the chair. Her anticipation curled at the edges, like the blossom. Something had happened. Mrs. Moore didn't want to see her. Always, during the first minutes, Cynthia felt stiff, but today there was something different, an acid tang of hostility. She watched Mrs. Moore's small white hands stabbing at the embroidery. A fat red petal on a rose took shape. Suddenly Mrs. Moore laid her embroidery on her knee and looked at Cynthia, her small mouth hard.

"I don't know what you've been saying to your mother about me, Cynthia, but I am surprised that you could give her such a false idea! I've told you how lonesome I was in this town, and then instead of helping me make friends, you make your mother think — why, dreadful things!"

The words shouted incredibly about Cynthia, their impact blocking, for the moment, all sensation.

"I've been very nice to you, I'm sure, and then —" From the work-basket beside her, Mrs. Moore drew a letter. Cynthia saw the small, regular writing of her mother, pages of it! "Why, she accuses me of trying to draw you away from her, your own mother! I thought you were a nice, sensible girl." The letter rustled under Mrs. Moore's fingers. "Whatever have you said about me?"

"I haven't said anything —" Cynthia had to drive the words out.

"She says —" Mrs. Moore turned the letter — "that she's seen the silliest letters and notes — that I must be unscrupulous to allow a young girl to say such things to me. Now you can just tell your mother the truth. I haven't seen any silly letters! You haven't said anything to me!"

Cynthia crouched in her chair. She couldn't see Mrs. Moore plainly. She seemed to be growing larger, larger, covering the window, the world, while Cynthia shrank into a pinpoint of consciousness. Then the point exploded into waves of shame, hot, suffocating, blinding. Silly letters! Her mother had found those letters she had written — had read them —

"Cynthia! Don't sit there staring at me with your mouth open!" There were glints in the woman's eyes like the points of the scissors in her lap. "Did you hear what I said?" Her voice brought her back to normal size, and Cynthia could see her clearly again. "I want you to tell your mother exactly what we have talked about here. I won't have her suspecting me of — of all sorts of things! You should have told me she didn't like you to come. It's difficult enough in a strange town to get in with people without having a silly child hurting my reputation by pretending that I — well!" Mrs. Moore stopped, her eyelids twitching. "When I have just been so lonesome I was glad to have anybody to talk to, even a child!"

Cynthia stumbled up to her feet.

"I haven't pretended anything —" she began. She stopped because her throat ached.

"Of course I'll answer this letter. I'd like to talk with your mother, but since she wrote instead of dropping in —" Mrs. Moore pursed her lips into a tiny red dash.

25

Cynthia pressed her hands against her breast, a gesture instinct with protest against the stripping of herself. Her letters! All her dreams set down and hidden away —

"But I think it is only fair that you should tell her, too, that I haven't known anything about any unwholesome ideas you had!"

Then a strange thing happened to Cynthia, as though Mrs. Moore's words were knives cutting away the mystery and fragile dream-fabric the child had hung about the woman. She looked at Mrs. Moore and saw her as a woman old as her mother, a kind of starved suspiciousness in the large dark eyes, a cruel hungry little mouth, with a faint line of dark hair above the thin upper lip.

"I'm sorry mother wrote to you," she said. She was trembling under a pelting of rage. "She made a mistake. The letters weren't for you. I don't know — what you think I've pretended — why, it's too dreadful —"

"Of course you're too young to understand how serious it might look." Mrs. Moore's voice dropped from its rasp of accusation into mild complaint. "But in this town — when you know how I've wanted to make friends —"

Cynthia stood for a moment, while her rage moved within her in a convulsive tightening of her muscles. She thought: "It's you that's pretended — to like me — and all the time —" Then, with a little "Oh-h," between a sob and a laugh, she ran out of the room, through the hall, away from the terrible house.

Around the corner she stopped her mad run; someone was coming toward her. She couldn't breathe very well, but she pressed her lips against the sobs, and walked at the edge of the sidewalk, her head averted. She wanted to hide. Perhaps a broken heart showed! The boy passed her, whistling, and she was alone again, moving slowly past the small drab houses with their hostile, curtained windows.

A tiny wild thing, with bright eyes and hot breath, turning, twisting, to escape from the pit into which it had been thrust; twisting until it dropped, confused and dizzy. No way out. Curious adult eyes staring into the pit. Her mother, reading the letters. Mrs. Moore, pursing her lips. "I thought you were a nice girl!" She couldn't go home. Her mother would ask her questions. But she had no other place to go.

Suppose she died. She would grow paler and paler, until finally the doctors said, despairing, "She cannot live." Then her mother would weep and beg her forgiveness, and Mrs. Moore would come to kneel beside her — No, she wouldn't! Mrs. Moore didn't care. That was the astounding discovery. She had just pretended. The consoling vision fell away from her, and she was back on the street with the staring windows. She hated these grown-ups, with their power and their airs of wisdom! Her hands clutched at the pockets of her coat, and hot tears splashed down her cheeks. At any rate, she had told Mrs. Moore the letters weren't for her. Had she lied? Had her mother written much about them? They weren't to Mrs. Moore! Mrs. Moore was a woman with hard, shiny eyes and cruel voice, a woman who said queer things about her reputation. The letters were written to — Cynthia stopped, brushing the tears away from her face with impatient, grimy fingers. She felt cold, as though she had come, suddenly, into a strange, barren land, a country stripped of the bright wonder of her dreams. For she

27

knew, reluctantly, that she had written those letters to no one outside herself, that she had had no friend.

Shivering, tense, she came to the door of her home. Her fingers turned the knob silently, and she stepped into the hall. She heard her mother in the parlor, talking, in the deliberate, formal tone which meant a caller. She climbed the stairs, her feet silent on the carpeted steps.

She left her door ajar; then she could hear if someone came upstairs. The small white bed, the white dresser and little rocker, the pictures tacked on the blue walls, surrounded her with a curious stupid familiarity. She knelt by the dresser and tugged at the bottom drawer. Under the piles of clothes and stockings she fumbled. Her fingers touched something smooth, drew back, and then dragged out a small cardboard box tied with a blue ribbon. Its edges grew prismatic through quick tears of self-pity. She had thought them beautiful, these letters. Into them she had written all the strange feelings of the past months, the things she could never have said aloud, the lines of poetry she had liked. Desecrated now. Silly, silly! The word screamed around her.

She listened a moment at the head of the stairs. Her mother's voice came at intervals, a polite, suave tone. Silently Cynthia crept down the rear stairs into the kitchen. With infinite caution against noise, she lifted a lid of the range, crammed the box into the red coals, and waiting until it blackened, curled, flamed up, replaced the lid.

She stood trying to hear the faint crackle of the paper when her mother appeared at the door.

"Oh, you're home, Cynthy." She hesitated. "You didn't stay long."

Then the little trapped wild thing in Cynthia saw a crack of escape, darted for it. Her mother wanted to know what had happened! She needn't tell her. She would never tell her!

"No, not so very," she said. Her eyes, bright with defiance, met her mother's inquiring gaze.

"Well, did Mrs. Moore say anything?" Impatience, embarrassment in her mother's face.

"Oh, we talked," said Cynthia. She trembled with her new triumph. Her mother couldn't ask her, plainly, what had happened there! She would never tell her. Mrs. Moore could write her, if she wanted to.

* * * * *

Cynthia had, during the last few years, been rebellious often enough, but always when her passion had ebbed she had waited, with a hot, dry sensation in her mouth, and a heavy, wretched lump somewhere inside her, until her mother had forgiven her, soberly, and she had promised to be good again. This was different. Her excitement had no fear in it. She had made herself an impregnable retreat. For the first time she was sharply a person, thrilling with the bitter taste of separation from other people. The frayed ropes which had bound her had broken at last. Something in her no one could touch, could demand — not even her mother.

"Some day, Cynthia" — Cynthia knew the futility under the sharp words — "you will realize that your mother is your best friend. If you wish to be secretive and stubborn —"

A demon of glee danced about Cynthia. Her mother wanted to know what had happened! She couldn't ask

29

outright, because she couldn't say, "I read your silly letters, and I want to know what that woman said!" Again the gleeful, bitter taste of separate identity. For the first time she had something which no one could enter, could wrest from her. She kept her refuge of silence. Her mother, with a grave, disapproving look, came past her into the kitchen. Cynthia's heart gave a frantic leap; would she open the range, and see the charred papers? But she went on to the table under the window.

After a moment Cynthia went slowly through the dining room. When she had hung away her hat and coat in the hall closet, she stood at the window. The spring dusk blurred the ugly yards and muddy road into gray mystery. Cynthia felt cold and empty. "Elaine the fair, Elaine the beautiful" — dying of unrequited love — that wasn't real. She had been playing. She had done with that game, now, just as she had put away her dolls — when was it, a year ago? And in its place she had — she pressed her arms fiercely about her body — she had herself, Cynthia, separate, apart — growing up!

ALLEY WAYS

Cynthia hurried between the sheeted counters toward the door. She had lingered so long that the other clerks had gone, and Mr. Bell himself stood, just shaking off his managerial airs, in final directions to the basement man. He unlatched the door for Cynthia, who slipped past him with a grave good night. Within her gravity, though, hung streamers of delight; she was proud of Mr. Bell's black-haired suaveness, proud of it as something belonging to her, since he managed the store where she clerked; she delighted in her own importance in being thus let out of the secretive, closed shop. She glanced down the street to see whether anyone had noticed her emergence. At the sight of a girl loitering before the windows a few stores ahead she shivered, a forbidden streamer fluttering out. Queenie wouldn't take a hint, then. Cynthia walked slowly toward her, framing bits of self-defense. She had waited as long as she could; Queenie should have been blocks ahead of her. Instead, there she was, dropping into step beside her, a sick furtiveness glinting in wide, blue eyes.

"If you're tryin' to shake me, say so."

"Don't be silly!" exclaimed Cynthia, and the relief that chased off the furtiveness in Queenie's face banished her own faint resolve. She couldn't strike at her brutally, as her mother had demanded.

"Was it Bell kept you? You're awful' late."

"No. I — I couldn't come earlier."

They swung off the main street, Queenie struggling to keep step.

"If you tried to shake me now, after all I told you, —" her plaintive voice came over Cynthia's shoulder, — "I don' know what I'd do."

"Has anything happened?"

"Say, you don't need to run home, do you?" She plucked at Cynthia's arm, and with a little laugh Cynthia slackened her stride.

"Nothing's happened, Queenie?" she repeated.

"I saw him."

"Queenie! Again! Where?"

"This noon. He was waiting — down near the river."

"What did you do?"

"I acted like I didn't see him; and then — I tried to run; and then I got home somehow."

"You didn't talk to him?"

32

Queenie shook her head, her eyes staring into Cynthia's in dogged appeal.

"Good for you! O Queenie, good for you!" Cynthia's cheeks flushed.

"Well, you said you'd help me if I didn't talk to him."

"And you said you couldn't help it; and now you've proved you could." Cynthia's voice rang out in young triumph.

"I was afraid he'd wait for me tonight." Queenie glanced at the warehouses they were passing. "He turns me all to water. You don't know."

"I knew, if you wanted to do it, you could." Cynthia nodded wisely at Queenie. She glowed with her triumph; she had projected her own strength into this girl. "I'll walk down your street with you, and then if he comes —" She ended with a note of scorn.

"I keep thinking it's him I see."

"Don't think about him. He isn't worth it."

"He ain't worse'n most men."

"But if you think about other things —"

"What things?" Queenie's full lips twitched. "You can pretend you ain't thinking about it, but it's right there." She seized Cynthia's arm, a curious gurgle in her throat. "See! Is that him?" She pulled Cynthia to a stop in front of a little drugstore, peering in between the red and blue bottles.

"Don't stop and stare!" Cynthia jerked her along.

" 'T wasn't." Queenie turned her face slowly back to Cynthia. Little blotches of color showed under the soft, pale cheeks. She clung to Cynthia's arm, pressing it against her body. "Oh, I don' know how to bear it!"

A strange tremor moved through Cynthia. She dragged her arm free.

33

"Don't act so here on the street," she said gently. "Someone will notice you."

They were almost to the river. A wagon passed them, the pitch of its rumble changing hollowly as it came to the wooden bridge.

"You see," Cynthia went on as the girls reached the bridge, "it is wicked to feel like that, now you know he has a wife." Queenie's emotion was strange wine on her lips, dizzying her.

"I didn't know that when I got to loving him." Queenie stared down at the muddy, sluggish current.

Cynthia grew stern.

"You do know now," she said; "so you must stop."

A group of workmen straggled past them, one of them grinning, teeth white in the grime and tan of his face.

"From the yards," said Queenie, pointing to the tracks across the river.

"You aren't listening."

"Oh, I hear you. But what am I going to do?" Queenie clung to the rail. "Sometimes —" she flung up her hand — "I think I'll jump in. Living so handy to the river, I think of it."

"Nonsense!" Cynthia drew her again into a slow walk. "Don't you talk that way. You've got a job, and there are lots of things for you to do."

"Job! It's all right for you to talk, coming in for two weeks of the sale. How'd you like selling notions all the time? 'Yes, 'm, these are five cents. No; them are ten.' Fine way to live, ain't it!"

"I think it's fun."

"You got something else ahead. Would you stay doing it?"

"Well," — Cynthia hesitated, — "the family wouldn't let me. It was all I could do to make them let me do it these

34

two weeks. But I think I'd like it. You could get to be head of a department."

"Get laid off for the dull season!"

They had reached the end of the bridge, and Cynthia stopped impatiently. Queenie's apathy roiled the clear water of her wisdom — a lip wisdom that she echoed unquestioningly.

"If you won't make any effort yourself!" she cried. Queenie sucked in the corners of her mouth; an incongruous dimple flickered in one cheek. Her huge sailor-hat had slipped back, and her fair hair lay in moist curls around her forehead and ears. She looked almost like a baby, thought Cynthia, pityingly, so that she hurried on. "But of course you want to. Now let's think. If you don't like the store, why not try something else?"

Queenie shook her head.

"I set out to be a private secret'ry, but I didn't have the mem'ry. I saved up, and took a course, but I couldn't learn it."

"Well," — Cynthia walked on, — "there must be something. I'll think about it."

They came to an alley squeezing between old sheds.

"Would you —" Queenie hesitated — "would you have time to come down a piece with me?"

The two stepped into the dingy passage, Queenie shrinking close to Cynthia.

"I always feel he might step out the other side of this."

There was nothing beyond the sheds, though, but a mud path close along the river, with a cluster of shacks.

"Third one's where I live," said Queenie, defiantly. " 'T aint much and it's full of kids. You better go back now." She clutched at Cynthia's arm. "You won't shake me, will you? Just feelin' there's somebody knows, gives me more spunk."

"Of course not. I'll help you, Queenie." Cynthia flung up her head, her voice vibrating in her throat. The squalor of the houses by the river, the strange, dirty alley, this soft, trembling Queenie — all became an entrancing mystery lying in her hands for her to shape. "Good night," she whispered. "I'll see you tomorrow."

She ran back through the alley, half expecting to be halted by a stranger, by him, perhaps.

As, breathless, she reached the street she heard a loud "Cynthia!" and there was her father pulling up his horse. She climbed in beside him, her "Hello, Father!" as nonchalant as her quick breath permitted. Confusion whirled within her for a moment, and then quieted enough to be recognized as despair. What were all her defenses, now that she had been seen coming out of the alley itself?

"Little late, aren't you?" her father asked.

"Why, not much."

"Your mother asked me to pick you up."

In the pause that followed, Cynthia set her chin, her eyes on the smooth, rapid motion of Daffy's flanks. She wouldn't say a thing. He could go ahead, if he had to. After a moment he did, casually.

"What's so attractive about that girl, Cynthy?"

"I tried to get rid of her to-night —" At her father's glance a flush prickled in her eyelids, and she went on: "I did. I waited until the store was locked up. She was still hanging around. She begged me to go down the alley."

"Well," — he touched up the horse, — "you've had enough of the store. Your mother needs you around the house."

36

A lurch of the road-cart threw Cynthia against her father, and she saw, incredulously, the lines down his lean cheeks deepen. He wasn't joking. He had swung over to the other side, then. She had lost her amused ally. "But, Father, the sale lasts all this week. I can't stop." "Bell's won't go out of business. If you won't play fair, you can't do what you want to." "It isn't playing fair to go back on somebody that needs you." Her father looked around at her. "You can't do that girl any good. She's a poor lot. Your mother told you to drop her. That's all there is to it."

He turned the horse under the elm trees of the drive, and walked her in silence to the steps of the house. There he waited for Cynthia to get out. She stood for an instant by the wheel, her eyes entreating him. But with a flick of the lines he said:

"I'll just tell your mother you aren't going to work any more," and Cynthia, lagging up the steps, knew bitterly he meant that as a concession, the only one he could make her.

Supper was ready; she could hear her mother moving about the kitchen.

"I'll be right down," she called halfway up the stairs.

As she splashed her eyes with cold water she pressed her fingers against them, so that the blood in the tips pounded on the eyeballs.

"Oh, I hate them!" she thought. "I won't go down!"

Then Robert called shrilly:

"Cynthy! Supper!" and she went slowly down to the dining-room.

Through the desultory supper-talk she was aware of her mother's gaze drifting about her, retreating if she looked up restively. Robert, eyeing her over his bread and butter, announced between bites:

"Huh, Cyn looks sick of her job."

"I am not!" Cynthia flashed at him, and winced as her mother replied:

"Hush, Robert! Cynthia is tired."

Later, in a dark corner of the porch, Cynthia looked into her black mood. It was all distorted images of herself: the self Mr. Bell would think her for "quitting her job," when she had said she could work two weeks; the self he would think her if he learned that she was being dragged away like a baby; the self — this all a shattered image — that Queenie would think her when she failed to appear in the morning, failed to keep that promise to stand by her. Gone were the bright images she loved of herself as a person of independence, as a superior saleswoman, and, brightest of all, sharpest, as a wise benefactor. Within the house voices droned, her father and mother talking. A little impotent rage blew through her, blurring the distorted images into a microcosm of humiliation. The screen door opened, and Cynthia, at the sight of her mother's figure, large in the dusk, drew back into her corner, a hard shell closing to about her heart.

"Cynthia?"

"Yes."

"Oh, there you are." She settled into a chair near Cynthia, rocking leisurely. "Your father says you aren't going to the store any more."

Cynthia's shell strained altogether.

"You haven't been yourself since you were there. It's too hard work."

"Other girls do it," cried Cynthia.

"They have to. You don't."

38

There was a silence, in which Cynthia felt tiny flames of antagonism lick out from her contracted heart. Then her mother spoke again in the tone of one offering diversion to a sulky child.

"Rachel Meredith came in this afternoon. She said her dresses had come home. Why don't you go over now to see them, if you aren't too tired? You won't have much more chance to see Rachel."

Cynthia stirred in her chair. She did want to see Rachel. She wanted to refuse her mother's suggestion, but after a moment of perversity she knew she wished more to see Rachel.

"I might go over," she admitted.

"Don't stay too late, although you won't need to get up early tomorrow."

Until she was out of sight of the house Cynthia walked slowly; then she quickened her steps until she was almost running. The huge elms gathered the night in pools under their branches; waves of light ran out from the windows she passed, breaking into curious white foam on rose bushes or dropping on smooth, pale lawns. The self of humiliation drifted away from her. Rachel would help her, would know what to do for Queenie. The thought of Rachel sang through her — tall, sweet Rachel, with white, light-touching hands.

She crept noiselessly across the grass to the side of the Meredith house. The French windows stood open to the screened porch, and just within one of them Rachel sat reading. Cynthia caught her breath in a second of hushed adoration; mystery lay about Rachel, like the soft light on her dark hair and graceful neck. Tonight and tomorrow she could sit there reading; then she would be gone, changed. The thought of the strange man who was to come Friday to marry Rachel stirred in Cynthia jealous

39

wonder. She wanted Rachel to look up, to see her standing there. Suddenly, with the breath of some warm night scent, Queenie seemed to press against her, quivering, imploring — Queenie in love, too. Her image dimmed the mystery about Rachel, and Cynthia moved impatiently away from such disloyalty. At the sound Rachel glanced up, and, with a soft "Cynthia!" came out to the edge of the veranda.

"Don't stand there staring, little moth!" she laughed. "Come in!"

Her voice was a warm rain of confusion falling deliciously upon Cynthia. She stumbled on the step, and then Rachel drew her inside the screens, laying an arm about her shoulders, and led her up the broad stairway to her own room. There was mystery here, too, in the disorder of the quiet, spacious chamber, in half-filled trunks, and piles of soft colors and textures on low chairs. Two nights more, and the beautiful disorder would be gone.

"Sit here, child." Rachel pushed to the floor a mass of tissue-paper, and Cynthia crouched on a corner of the couch.

"They must all be packed tomorrow, and I knew you'd wish to see them."

Cynthia watched mutely, her eyes on the slender hands which caressed the fabrics, shaking out folds of silk, touching bits of embroidery. Rachel slipped her arms into a bright mandarin coat, and wheeled in front of Cynthia. Incongruously, Queenie seemed to fling up her hands there, clumsy, short-fingered. Rachel, turning back to Cynthia, paused.

"What is it?" she asked.

The coat dropped from her shoulders, and she stepped near the couch. Cynthia shook her head; Queenie had no place here.

"I believe you'd like me not to be married, little dumb thing!" Rachel touched Cynthia's cheek with cool fingers. "Is that it?"

"Oh, no; no!"

"Want to be rid of me, eh?"

"Rachel!" At Rachel's laugh Cynthia flushed. Perhaps Rachel guessed how she reveled in the exotic pain of losing her.

"There, I won't torment you. Come, we'll go out on the porch. This is all, except loads of silver. Mother can show you that, if you like, afterward."

On the veranda again, Rachel sank into her hammock, and bade Cynthia pull her chair close.

"Now," she said lazily "tell me what you've done today."

"I can't go back to the store." Cynthia plucked at the fringe of the hammock. "Father saw me — coming out the alley where Queenie lives. She's that girl, you know."

"I thought you decided last night to avoid her."

Cynthia drew her hand hastily away.

"She — needs somebody," she protested.

"O Cynthia," Rachel's voice rallied her, "your heart's too great for the world. That little alley girl doesn't need my Cynthia."

"But I can help her."

"Cynthia dear, Lottie used to live down there near the river. I asked her if she knew these McQuades."

"Well." Cynthia was hostile. Whatever that hired girl knew did not matter.

41

"This Queenie has a bad name. Her mother can do nothing with her."

"It's a stepmother. And, Rachel, she wants to — to do what's right. I know."

Rachel reached for Cynthia's hand, held it in her cool, firm grasp.

"It's you that's good, dear. You can't understand yet. You can't alter mud. You just get smirched yourself."

Cynthia held herself rigid against the sweet thrill of Rachel's touch.

"But suppose — you fell in love," — she sought for tangible form to give her confused thoughts, — "and then — he was married. Wouldn't it be hard?"

"Cynthia," said Rachel, releasing her hand, "you are an absurd child. If the girl were decent, she wouldn't be in love with a married man."

For a shivering moment Cynthia sat silent. Bending over a deep, lovely pool to touch it, she had found it polished glass. Then Rachel, with a sudden movement, drew her out of her chair to her knees by the hammock. The bewildering sweetness of Rachel's arms around her, of Rachel's throat against her hot cheek, sent that moment scuttling away, an ugly spider, to some remote corner of her being. She needn't know it was there. With a little sob she relaxed into the fragrant darkness.

"Don't think about it." Rachel's lips brushed her ear. "We have so few hours left. You are worn out — that horrid store!"

Think? She could think of nothing with Rachel lavishing light hands about her. Cynthia, sitting by the swaying hammock, felt the mystery creep about her, too. Rachel was so rich in love she could pour it out until the swimming joy became pain within you.

42

When Cynthia came slowly up the walk to her own house, voices on the porch ceased, and the red star of her father's cigar glowed out. "Yes, the things were very nice," she said in a vague way, moving on toward the door.

"Going to bed?"

"Yes. Good night."

Later, lying in bed, she heard that interrupted talk picked up again. She was too drowsy to care. With her mind full of the drifting images at the border of sleep, she was sinking, sinking, when, unguarded, out scuttled the horrid spider of doubt, rousing her to full wakefulness. Her mother and Rachel had talked that very day. Rachel had connived with her mother. There was surely something wrong in such easeful dispensing with Queenie. But Rachel's good-night kiss was there on her lips, seducing her to languor, and she slept.

The next morning she bent to household tasks with eager humility. She was unconsciously trying to force herself back to an old order of things, as though only thus could she be sure of loyalty to Rachel, of matter-of-fact tranquility at home. Her father was to stop at Bell's to say she wouldn't be down. Who would be given her counter? And Queenie — she saw her fumble with the cord of a parcel, count change into some customer's outstretched hand, always with her eyes toward the door, watching for her. At her mother's approach her thoughts would scatter, a swarm of flies driven from a bit of refuse, to gather black as soon as she was left alone.

Toward noon she put on her hat and sought out her mother.

"I'm going after my money," she said stubbornly.

"Mr. Bell might not be in this afternoon."

Her mother lifted her eyes from the white stuff she was sewing. For a second her needle continued its little pricking sound along a seam.

"I wanted you to try on this skirt," she suggested.

"You want it for Rachel's wedding, don't you?"

"I'll be right back." Cynthia fled.

The street was hot and still. The shadows huddled close about the trees, and the sweetish odor of tar swam in the glare. Cynthia's hurrying body sucked in the heat, grew heavy with it; but the discomfort gave her a dim relief. When she came at last to the bridge she stopped, peering off at the gray huddle of shacks. A breath from the river touched her moist forehead, and she looked down at the water, above which hung a wavering glow like molten air. Then she went on more slowly until she stopped again inside the doors of Bell's store.

It seemed dark and cool after the street, the aisles stretching back empty, interminable. She made her way between the counters, a dull sense of severance moving in her. The woman behind the silks nodded to her; she could see Mr. Bell's sleek head over the office partition.

Someone seized her arm. Queenie, with reproachful, swollen eyelids, made a grimace of caution toward the office, and drew Cynthia into the shelter of the tall thread-cases.

"I thought you wasn't ever coming."

"I can't work any more."

Queenie's lips twitched in her pallid face.

"Has a bad name." Cynthia seemed to hear Rachel's low voice. Poor Queenie! She looked as if she had melted a little and sagged down.

"Why not?" Queenie thrust her face close. "Is it — me? They won't have you seeing me?"

44

"They think the work's too hard." Cynthia's quick words fell back from Queenie's grin of contempt.

"Oh, I know; I ain't such a fool. You're too good." She leaned heavily on the counter, her eyelids growing redder. "Well, Bell's kicked me out, too. 'Won't need your services, Miss McQuade, after tonight.' They's just two things left." She broke off at the approach of a customer, who looked curiously at the two girls, fingered some ribbons, and trailed on. Cynthia waited tensely. "One's the river, th' other's him. Anyhow, he wants me."

"I'll ask Mr. Bell." Cynthia's fingers clenched into Queenie's arm. "When he knows I'm going to leave —"

Queenie's pale eyes hung on Cynthia's an instant. "Oh, you needn't bother." She edged away.

Had she felt that echoing speech — "You can't alter mud"? Cynthia drooped. Her power had run out of her; she had somehow lost her grip on Queenie. With a shrug Queenie tucked her blouse into her tight belt, and presented herself to the customer who had drifted back.

After an irresolute moment Cynthia made a rush toward the office. Awkward, aware of the dust on her shoes, she seated herself by Mr. Bell's desk. He looked up from his papers.

"Yes, Miss Bates?"

"I just came for my salary, Mr. Bell."

"Oh, yes. Your father stopped in this morning. So you've had enough of salesmanship?" He smiled, and Cynthia saw him changed to the Mr. Bell of church socials, his authority dropping away.

"They think so," she confided.

"Next time you want a job," — he pulled open a drawer, — "I'll give you a recommendation." He counted out three half-dollars. "Up to last night, wasn't it?"

Cynthia drew her finger along the edge of the desk. Into her manner came an alloy of flattery. Instinctively, to gain her request, she sought to please his suave maleness.

"Mr. Bell, there's something I wanted to ask you." Her breath fluttered. "As long as I have to — resign," — she offered that phrase as a small jest, and at his smile hastened on, — "couldn't you keep Queenie McQuade on? She needs work, oh, very much! She'll do her best."

Mr. Bell's smile was swallowed up in a return of his manager air.

"She's not an efficient clerk," he said shortly. He dropped the three coins into Cynthia's lap, and as she gathered them into her hand, added: "I'm sorry she's presumed upon your being in the store. I told your father and Miss Meredith this morning I regretted it. We don't mean to hire such girls."

Cynthia shrank away from the curiosity under his heavy eyebrows.

"They spoke to you — father and Rachel Meredith?"

"Just a word."

Cynthia stumbled to her feet.

"She must have work. She hasn't done anything." Did she say the words or only attempt them?

"Don't you bother your pretty head about her, Miss Bates. You can see it isn't fair to our patrons or our other clerks."

Then with a little nod he had dismissed her. Her furtive glance as she hurried from the store disclosed no glimpse of Queenie. Ducking across the street, she stopped in the shelter of the wooden Indian in front of the tobacco shop. No Queenie stalking her. Slowly she walked on in the swimming heat, the world and her own inner self swooning in a sort of suspended life.

46

When she dragged herself into the house, the glistening pallor of her face brought a sharp order from her mother.

"You lie down. I shouldn't have let you traipse downtown in this heat. This is the last bit of your foolishness."

She lay on the couch in the library. The shrill of locusts outside and the clatter of dishes in the dining-room seemed remote and unreal.

Doubling down the crooked ways of sleep, she sought for Queenie, while something formless and horrible pursued her. Its tentacles reached for her at her very heels. She tried to scream. It clutched her shoulder, and she wrenched herself free of dream and sleep, to find her mother looking down at her.

"You'd better have some lunch, Cynthia. It's late."

The rest of that day Cynthia gave herself with wistful docility to her mother's suggestions. She stood before the mirror while her mother knelt to adjust the folds of the white dress, a tall, thin girl with drooping shoulders.

"There, that's the best I can do." Her mother rose stiffly. "You don't seem to like it."

"Yes, I do, Mother. It's pretty." Cynthia let the dress slide to the floor and stepped out of the white pile, a flush touching her cheeks. She felt the somber weight of ingratitude that her mother should kneel there, working for her, while she had no joy even in the dress.

"If you'd just fill out a little —" Her mother's eyes were on her shoulders. "After the wedding you've got to rest up. You're like a rail."

Cynthia drew her gingham dress hastily over her head.

After supper, to Robert's glee, she offered to play checkers. Something inside her lay numb, with faint

pricklings, like a cramped foot. As she bent over the black
and yellow squares she heard her mother say:

"After the excitement of the wedding she'll be all
right."

Rachel's lover had come that afternoon. Cynthia was
full of fierce relief that there was no chance of seeing
Rachel again.

But at last she walked slowly, in order that she might
not grow warm and red, under the elms and up the path to
the Meredith house. Mrs. Meredith herself opened the
door. Unexpectedly she kissed Cynthia, sighing, "Your
turn some day soon." For the first time Cynthia saw her
as Rachel faded and hardened by the years. She led
Cynthia into the parlor, heavy with the sweetness of
many roses. Cynthia was the only outsider. She sank into
a chair, pulling her feet close to the rockers; Rachel's
aunt, in stiff gray silk, her father, florid and strident, the
minister in formal black, regarded her solemnly, almost
hostilely. Then, after a long moment, Rachel stood
between the curtains. Her eyes sought Cynthia's over the
great cluster of roses in her arms, caressed her swiftly,
and lifted to the man beside her. Back flooded the
beautiful mystery, and Cynthia abandoned herself to it.
She scarcely saw the man, after one glance at his blond
head over Rachel's. She saw only Rachel's face, the rise
and fall of the lace at her breast. Incredibly soon it was
over; Rachel lifted her face to the man, and a jealous
ecstasy racked Cynthia at their grave kiss. Rachel turned
to her people, laughing; her arms held Cynthia for an
instant.

Presently the machine whirled up to the door, and in a
flash Rachel was gone, slim, tailored, beside the straight,
proud figure of her husband.

Cynthia started slowly toward home, Rachel's roses filling her arms, their fragrance swimming up in the heat. Insidiously another odor mixed with theirs, until, with a shiver, Cynthia halted. Stripped quivering from her, naked, rose the hidden impulse. She must see Queenie. Unless she did, she couldn't endure this beauty. It wasn't fair. Forgetting the heat, shaking away the little thought of her mother waiting to hear about the wedding, she turned down the long street to the river.

Even at the entrance to the alley she did not hesitate. The third house, Queenie had said. It stood nearer the river than the others, down a sloping bank. Cynthia walked straight to the door, the roses drooping against her dress. Scraggly hens scurried off the doorstep. Inside, at her knock, came a scuffling sound, a smart slap, followed by a child's cry. The door opened, and a woman, wiping reddened arms on her drab wrapper, faced her.

"How do you do?" Cynthia peered past her into a room full of the sour smell of wash-water. "I'm Cynthia Bates." She tried to smile against the woman's grim stare. "Is — is Queenie here?"

"What do you want of her?"

Cynthia shrank back, her roses and white dress suddenly strident with mockery. The woman snatched at a buzzing fly, and shook her skirts clear of the clutching child who had crept to her feet. He pursed his dirty little mouth for a cry, and she jerked him into her arms.

"What you want?" she repeated.

"I knew her in the store."

"Oh, you're that one! Well, she ain't here."

"Is she working somewhere?"

"Working! Her! Folks won't keep her. Expectin' us to feed her — a grown woman."

49

The woman returned to her tubs, setting the child on a chair. Cynthia saw round eyes, pale like Queenie's, staring at her from behind the tubs.

"She isn't here?" she persisted.

"I don't know where she is, and, what's more, I don't want to." The woman broke into irritated volubility. "I says to her, if you can't work, you needn't eat. Crazy about the fellows she was, wanting to dress up fine and run with 'em. I stood it till she mixed up with a married man; then I says, 'this is enough of you.' "

"Where did she go?" Cynthia asked slowly.

"She ain't been here since yesterday morning. She needn't show her face here again."

Cynthia climbed the slope, the roses slipping from her arms. She glanced back once. The baby had crept to the step, and sat gravely pulling the red petals from one of them. She felt curious eyes nibble at her from the other shacks.

As she entered the alley, she looked back at the river, catching a sob at the sight of a bit of white. Only a paper sluggishly drifting; not Queenie's round, pleading face.

In the alley the air hung stagnant, rotting with the old buildings. Queenie was gone, Rachel was gone. She came out to the glare of the street, and after a second's pause went on to the bridge. Leaning on the railing, she forced her eyes back to the squalid shore. For the first time she saw it without a hovering vision of herself as ministering angel. There it lay. Somewhere else Rachel was hurried off to shining happiness. And Queenie —

A grinding moment, and stark and undisguised that dormant thing within her stood up. They had done it, Rachel and the rest — pushed Queenie back into her mud. Under goodness lay that festering.

She would confront them with that terrible accusation. Her head high, she started swiftly toward her home. Presently her steps lagged again. The hard brilliance of her judgment dimmed. They would only repeat the things they had said. With her white skirts swinging limply about her ankles she came to the quiet, comfortable houses, in one of which she lived. A strange aloofness filled her. If she tried to tell them, her father and her mother, they would drag her back, shut her in safety, keep her cabined, *good.* She would keep silent.

She came to the steps of the house, a pale light in her tired face. Her quest had begun, secret, bewildering.

Original illustration for "Alley Ways" in *Century*, February 1918.

GROPING

"Was that really true, what you said?"

"What?" Cynthia leaned against the wall, tucking her gray kimono about her feet. From that position she could watch the girl who stood before the mirror, braiding her dark hair. She could even catch glimpses in the glass of the girl's face and firm neck, very white as it rose from the folds of the scarlet bathrobe. "What did I say?" she asked again, although she knew exactly what Mary meant.

"That you'd never kissed any — man?"

"Yes, it's true." Cynthia clasped her thin arms about her knees. "I didn't suppose you did unless you were engaged."

"Bless the child!" Cynthia caught a flash of white teeth in the mirror as Mary flung a long braid over her shoulder. "How'd anybody ever know she wanted to be engaged?"

"I've not been engaged," said Cynthia.

Into her eyes and stubborn little mouth had come an intensity which rested in curious presaging on the thin, sober face with its high forehead. She was thinking that here was another of the things she didn't know about, another of the things she had never talked about until tonight. She hadn't talked much tonight; she had listened. The little dormitory room had taken on an atmosphere of midnight confessional, with youth offering all it knew of life, before the other girls, friends of Mary, had pulled themselves sleepily from their chairs and couch corners and said good-night. Shut in alone with Mary, warm, vivid Mary, Cynthia expanded delicately, pushing out from bonds of reticence. Perhaps Mary would tell her more about love and being engaged after they were in bed. She thrust the question aside, and returned to her delight in Mary's intricate preparations for the night. The crisp rustle of the red ribbon Mary was tying about her head pleased Cynthia; she loved the curve of the white arms, with the loose sleeves flaming back from them.

Mary dropped her brushes and turned.

"There! I'm ready. Tired waiting?"

Cynthia jumped from the couch to help eagerly in the process of despoiling it of cover and reducing it to an ordinary bed.

"Pretty narrow," said Mary, as she slid one of the cushions into a pillow-case. "Guess we can manage, though."

"Oo — it's cold!"she cried, pushing a window open and running back to the bed. "Turn off the light there and hurry!"

In the darkness Cynthia climbed between the covers, trying to make herself as small as possible at the edge of the cot.

"Cuddle up, Goosey!" exclaimed Mary, thrusting an arm under Cynthia's shoulders, and Cynthia thrilled to breathlessness in the warm embrace.

"Didn't anybody ever try to kiss you?" demanded Mary after a moment.

"Once." For some reason Cynthia was glad she could say once, at least. "But I didn't like him to try."

Mary drew her more closely against herself, laying her free hand on Cynthia's cheek.

"How cool your hand is." Cynthia snuggled against it.

"Dear!" murmured Mary, and then, impetuously, "You ought to know how it feels, I think." She lifted Cynthia's face to hers, and her full lips closed on Cynthia's. Cynthia lay very still, but within her slender, inert body something began to whirl and whirl, up to the sweet soft lips of Mary. Suddenly, with a shiver, she pulled away, hiding her face against Mary's throat.

"It's like that," Mary whispered, "love is, only far, far more wonderful. You — you don't mind?" she asked, as Cynthia trembled in her arms.

"Oh, no!" Cynthia drew away from her. "But it frightens me."

"That's just that you didn't know," said Mary. Under the practical tone was a note of uneasiness. "I thought you ought to know." She settled herself more deeply into the pillows. "There's so much a girl has to find out for herself. I did."

"I guess —" Cynthia felt toward Mary with a timid hand. "I guess I have a great deal to find out."

Mary seized her hand and pulled her again into the fragrant curve of her shoulder.

"You're a dear!" she said, and a moment later, sleepily, "If I were a man I'd love you." Her drowsy lips brushed Cynthia's forehead.

Cynthia clung to the hand, full of the delight and the pain of mysterious quickening. More wonderful, Mary had said, and instinct-driven, blind, she yearned for that promise of great wonder. She felt beneath her cheek the slow, regular breathing, as Mary slept. Something rustled. She raised her head cautiously; only the curtain blowing in against the desk. The cold wind tingled in her nostrils, and she dropped back into her shelter. The faint, sensuous odor of white flesh made her glow, and in the dark warmth she drowsed, her mind full of new imaginings that hurried after her into her dreams.

She woke the next morning with a start, wondering what it was she was trying to grasp. Suddenly she remembered; as she looked over at Mary, who was stirring reluctantly, she flushed. Then she pushed the thing away from her thoughts; it didn't belong to the bright morning, someway. Behind her thoughts, however, it still worked, so that she jumped out of bed without minding the chilly room, lowered the window, brought Mary her bathrobe, all in a mood of impersonal gratitude.

Breakfast in the big dormitory dining room was a hasty performance; after that Cynthia helped Mary straighten her room. Then she hurried into her coat and hat, while Mary, grumbling because she must spend the morning in a laboratory, gathered her notebooks.

"I'll walk to the car with you," she told Cynthia, "for a breath of air. Wish you lived in the dormitory instead of home."

They walked briskly across the campus, the snow crunching under their heels. Cynthia slipped her hand in Mary's arm with a little skip.

"Aren't things bright this morning!" she said. "Bright blue, bright black —" they were passing a line of pointed firs — "bright white!"

"Cold, too." Mary pulled her sweater about her throat. "Guess I'll run back here."

Cynthia looked up at her. She was wishing she had Mary's bright color; it fitted into the clear winter day.

"I've had a beautiful time," she said. Then she added quickly, "I'm going to the Assembly tonight."

"With Clark?" Mary's eyes met hers, flashed sudden meaning, and dropped.

"Yes." Cynthia hesitated. At a distant rumble she withdrew her arm. "There's my car. I'll have to run. Goodbye!"

Breathless, she dropped into a seat at the rear of the yellow car which connected the college with the town. She bent her head, adjusting her hat and searching her purse for a handkerchief as several girls followed her into the car. In their furs and velvet hats they made her feel awkward; she didn't know them well, anyway. They seated themselves in seats ahead of her, and as the car jangled its starting bell, Cynthia relaxed comfortably. She could watch them now, without having to strain for some answer to their chatter. For a time she did watch them, wistfully; they were much cleverer than she, much prettier. One of them tucked up a lock of hair with a smoothly white-gloved hand, and Cynthia resented bitterly her own clumsy woolen gloves. Her usual solace, that she could outstrip them in her classes, failed her. They were all beautifully gowned young ladies, and she, outside the pale, a queer, awkward girl. She turned her face toward the frosty window. A whiff of air as the door behind her opened to admit a passenger caught her nostrils, and she slipped into the night before. Half guiltily she lingered a moment at the verge of definite recalling. Was it wicked, when it was so beautiful? Even if it was! Slowly she let herself down into the pool of memory, amazed that she could thrill so at things cool over night. Through the memories came, somehow, the last glance Mary had given her, and swift, uncalled pictures of Clark, the boy with whom she went occasionally to dances. The car's jerk as it swung into a switch aroused her, and she hurried off and up the short block to her home, whipping on an air of great nonchalance as she ran up the steps.

In the entry she stopped, to hang her coat and hat on the rack. As she opened the door into the hall she heard her mother's "Is that you, Cynthia?" and smelled the spicy odor of baking. She followed the voice into the kitchen.

"Well, you're here!" Her mother looked up from the pile of dishes she was drying, the habitual irritation of the tired house-keeper in her tone.

Cynthia glanced about the kitchen, with a vague expectation that she might find something changed; she felt as though she had been gone for a long time. Everything was quite the same, however, even to the oatmeal kettle soaking at the back of the range.

58

"I came right after breakfast," she defended herself against an imagined reproach.

"There's lots to do," replied her mother.

Cynthia took the long-sleeved apron from the hood and slipped her arms into it, turning for her mother to button it at the neck. She still had a feeling of remoteness; for a moment she had lost her continuity with the familiar routine of home life. Her mother patted her shoulder.

"Did you have a good time?" She put the question in a casual way, and Cynthia answered "Yes" in the same tone. "What shall I do?" she asked quickly, to prevent her mother's keen glance from developing into words.

"I don't know." Her mother sighed. "I've had a bad time with the range. There's everything to do."

"You go and sit down. Let me finish the dishes." Cynthia tried to brush her away from the table.

"No, indeed. If you're ready to work, you can see to the upstairs. And the sitting room's got to be brushed up. Was it a nice evening?"

Cynthia stopped in the doorway. "Very nice." In a little rush of pity for her mother she added, "And afterwards some of the girls came up to Mary's room and had a spread. The best cake! One of their mothers sent it. And they stayed and talked."

"So you did have a good time." Cynthia walked on into the dining room to hide the accusing flush which had run up into her face. Vaguely in her mind flashed the justification, "Mother doesn't want me to know anything. She thinks I'm just a little girl yet."

"Your father was put out because I let you stay," her mother was saying. "I told him you'd have a better time." The note of satisfaction deepened Cynthia's guilt, and she caught her lip between her teeth to keep back a reflection on her father.

Upstairs it was too cold for loitering. As Cynthia hurried about, spreading the fresh Saturday linen, setting the rooms in order, the pleasant indefinite mood of hands busy with a task and thoughts relaxed came to her. She swept, frosted the cake, helped with the lunch, and waved her mother off for a shopping trip. After she had cleared the luncheon things away, she hung her apron behind the door, and went through the quiet house to the library. Always she found it a pleasant adventure to be left alone in the house, and today! She curled up on the couch under the window, and with a little sigh, slipped into the warm flood of thoughts, of half-imaginings, of trembling dreams.

Late in the afternoon her mother returned, and the two hastened the preparations for supper. Cynthia was filling the water tumblers when her father, after much stamping of feet on the porch, came in. He was a stocky, heavy-shouldered little man, with an obstinate chin.

"Well!" he called out. "Thought you'd make us a little visit, did you?"

Cynthia frowned; it was difficult not to take her father's jokes too seriously. Through supper she was silent, eating listlessly, saying nothing, except in answer to questions. At the end, she pushed back her chair.

"I'll have to go and dress, mother."

"Why?" Her father gazed at her sharply. "Where are you going tonight?"

"Just to the Assembly," said the mother quickly.

"What for? You were out all last night."

"Last night," Cynthia said, struggling to speak in a very dignified tone, "was only the literary society at college. I haven't been to a dance for a long time."

"Humph. Who are you going with? That college fellow?"

"Yes." With an imploring glance at her mother, Cynthia fled up the stairs. She heard the protesting murmur of her mother's voice as she shut herself into her own room.

Her father certainly could be most unreasonable! But the deeper concern of dressing for the evening drove her father out of mind. First she brushed her fair hair, trying to fluff it out about her temples, and sighing as it proved too fine and soft. She tied a blue ribbon about it, leaning forward anxiously to peer at the result. She bit her lip; was the ribbon better than no ribbon? She decided to wear it, turning from her reflection with a flush of distress that she was so plain. From the closet she brought her blue dress, slipping it over her head, and fastening it with a little shrug of resignation. How could anyone be pretty who wore always the same clothes?

She waited an eager minute after the bell rang at eight. Perhaps it wasn't Clark. But she caught his "Good evening, Mr. Bates," and laughed to herself in pleasure at his deep formality. As she reached the foot of the stairs her mother sent her an anxious glance; she may have seen a hint of new flowering in the palely flushing face. Cynthia extended her hand, her eyes seeking the face of the boy, as though she thought to find it altered. He looked exactly as he always had; a clear, high-cheekboned face, with practical eyes and immature lips. Cynthia lingered in the doorway while her father asked a grave question concerning the tariff. She didn't hear Clark's answer; she thought, instead, how strong he looked, in his rough overcoat. Finally they were free to go. As they ran down the steps Clark seized her arm.

"I feel in jolly shape," he said. "Let's dance every dance."

Cynthia swung up to tiptoe and laughed. How he towered above her in the crisp dark! She could just see the outline of his face and the puffs of white steam his words made.

"Let's dance them all — together!" she exclaimed.

"That's the stuff. Let's hurry!"

The Assembly Hall was only a few blocks from the house, in the second story of an office building. Never had its windows shone more brightly, Cynthia was sure.

"Oh, I'm glad I can dance." Cynthia didn't know she had spoken aloud, until Clark pressed her arm more firmly.

"You feel good, too, don't you? Let's hurry!"

And they ran together up the wide wooden stairs to the second floor. The hour for the dancing lesson was just over, and a few of the more venturesome beginners were trying their steps on the polished floor, while the orchestra — a pianist and two 'cellists — tried their strings and hunted for the music of the first number of the real assembly. Cynthia hung her coat in the stuffy little cloakroom, sent a swift glance at her blue ribbon in the tiny mirror, for once indifferent to the other girls about her, and sped back to the hallway. Clark was there; she appraised quickly the other waiting males. Not one so tall, so straight, so clean as he, she thought.

It was a new, gay Cynthia that evening, so light that Clark declared she was nothing but the music itself. Her former sober delight in dancing had vanished; she herself did not know how she had come into possession of cajoleries, of daring words, of glances more daring, of eyes swiftly averted. When they swung out to the last waltz, Clark's hand tightened over hers.

"I wish we needn't stop." He bent over her, his breath fanning her cheek.

Cynthia's eyelids drooped; she was nothing but a reed through which the rhythmic motion ran. When the music stopped she went silently for her wraps, something within her hurting a little that the end had come.

They were both silent as they went out into the dark, frosty street. Cynthia shook her head at Clark's "Are you cold?" Her shoulder touched his arm, and in the dark her eyes widened. She slipped on the crusty walk, and Clark caught her hand. "You're shivering!" he exclaimed. "Here!" Then his arm was around her waist. Cynthia felt the rough coat almost against her cheek, felt her heart whirling within her. They crossed the street and mounted the steps of her home. At the door Cynthia pulled away.

"You — you might come in —" she said faintly.

"I might." Clark had a brusk nonchalance in his voice. "I'd like to get warm before I take my car."

They pushed the door softly open and entered. Cynthia's lips parted with a quick breath as she saw the empty sitting room. Her mother had not sat up for her.

"Let me take your coat." Clark's fingers were at her throat, unhooking the collar. She couldn't lift her eyes, but she wheeled, eluding his arms. She shook off the coat, and ran across the room.

"It's warmer over here by the register."

She faced him, leaning back against the wall, her hands outspread. With fluttering wings within her breast, she watched him as he came slowly toward her.

Something made her raise her heavy hands to pull the pins from her hat and drop it at her feet. The boy brushed it to one side and stood close to her. The fluttering wings ceased, and Cynthia thought in swift panic that she could even yet stop, could rush back to the old safe ground. This was happening because she had wished it. But Clark whispered, "Cynthia! Cynthia!" and she lifted her tender, wishing face. Then he had her in his arms, his lips eager against hers; her heart was molten quicksilver, escaping from her. Clark drew her down into a chair, and knelt beside her, lifting her quivering fingers to his lips and cheek. For a moment they remained thus, Cynthia in a silent ecstasy, pouring herself out through her fingertips. At a sound somewhere above them in the house, Clark got quickly to his feet.

"I suppose I ought to go," he said, listening uneasily. "It's pretty late."

Yes, it was late. Cynthia held her breath to listen. Her father might come to the stairs to call her up to bed. There was no sound again. But Clark moved toward the door.

"I'd better go."

Cynthia rose. Go? Now —? Her eyes alone made protest. At the door the boy stopped.

"Aren't you going to say good-night?" he asked softly.

Cynthia clasped her cold hands. He was going, and in that way!

"Good-night."

"That's not the way, Cynthia." He held his hands to her. "Here!"

She swayed, staring at him, held by a thread of sudden fear. With a sigh she broke the thread and ran to him, clinging to him, swinging up, up against his lips. Her own intensity frightened her, and she thought she was falling, until Clark released her, and she found herself standing in the entry, back in her own body. He was opening the door; she tried to say, "You will come again, soon —" but her lips would not move to the words.

"Good-night," he whispered, and was gone.

She set the night-latch, snapped off the light, and climbed the stairs quite without volition. A voice as she reached the hall above startled her so that she stumbled. "Did you lock the door, Cynthia?" "Yes," she answered, terrified lest her voice might betray her. But her mother called "Good-night," and Cynthia, gaining her room, pushed the door shut and waited in the darkness for her heart to cease pounding in her throat. She undressed rapidly, her mind yearning ahead to the kind shelter of her bed. Finally she lay there, straight and motionless. She would go over the evening moment by moment. Deliberately she returned to the beginning. Suddenly through her body flickered this new emotion, and she turned, hiding her face in the pillow, pulling herself against the bed to quiet the frightening quivers that ran through her. This — this must be love itself! She felt the pillow wet under her cheek; she hadn't known she had cried. She pressed her lips against it, moaning a little. It was wonderful, but terrifying, not to be understood. A crumpled leaf, she whirled up and up in the strong wind of desire she could neither see nor resist, until she slept.

Cynthia, the next day, struggled across the hours of a humdrum Sunday in a valorous attempt to pretend she was the same Cynthia. She was afraid someone would discover her secret; it glowed within her breast until she knew it must shine out and betray her. Not until after the late Sunday dinner, when under pretext of studying, she could retreat to her room with her books, was she free.

Sitting by her window, her chin propped on her hands, she drifted quite clear of the tedium of the day.

In the early winter evening the doorbell sounded in the house below. Cynthia jumped to her feet, and flinging open her door, ran to the head of the stairs. Could it be — it was! She heard Clark ask for her. She was downstairs in an instant, flashing past her father into the entry. In a moment she was again in the sitting room, her head thrown high.

"Clark can stay just a little while." Her voice defied her family. "We're going out for a short walk."

"You'll freeze to death," remarked her father, who was settling himself with his book.

"I've not been out all day." Cynthia spoke quickly. "I'll not be gone long."

She pulled a cap over her hair, wound a scarf about her throat, and shaking herself into her coat, joined Clark in the little entry.

"Quick!" she whispered. "Before they decide it's too cold."

Out in the street the lassitude of the day lifted from her. She walked provokingly at the far edge of the sidewalk, chattering of everything which drifted into her head. At the corner she turned into a street recently laid out, and but little built up. Clark, his hands in his pockets, gave sulky answers to her flitting queries. Then her chattering snapped off, and there was no sound but the cold talk of snow under their feet. A man passed them, peering over his shoulder before he disappeared into the night. The snow-covered fields were faintly luminous, with here and there a light picking out the window of a distant house. Cynthia felt Clark moving more closely toward her; they were alone in the bare little street. He touched her arm, and then their cold lips, clinging together, grew warm and moist. They walked on again, Cynthia's hand tight in Clark's. She glanced shyly at him; she was saying to herself, "I love you — I love you." Her lips tingled in the cold air; she felt radiant, as though her singing blood illumined her. She held her face up for a swift little kiss, laughing.

"I say —" Clark pressed her hand. "I've wanted to kiss you for a long time. I didn't know you were like this."

"Like what?" Cynthia wished she could see his face as he bent over her.

"Oh — liking to be kissed, you know."

"I never have!" Cynthia drew back from his face, her voice low with an instinctive pride in the value of her gift to him.

"What? Never? Oh, come!"

Cynthia was troubled; he shouldn't jest about this, even if he did wish to tease her. "Certainly not," she said, gravely.

"Oh, well! Most girls do."

"Do the girls you know?" Cynthia flung out the question as a recoil from the pain of his words.

"Why, yes." Clark paused, and then blundered ahead. "It's more fun going together then. Isn't it?"

Cynthia shrank away from his arm.

"You mean —" and her voice was thin and white like her breath in the winter air — "You mean you do it — for fun?"

"Well, don't you?" Clark demanded. "You let me," he added uncomfortably.

Cynthia was hurrying along, head bent; she wanted to escape the ogre of realization which pursued, close at heel.

"Don't go so fast!" Clark grasped her arm. "You — are you cross?"

"Cross?" Cynthia jerked out a little laugh. "I'm just cold. Let's hurry home. It seems much colder."

"Well, if you want to go home, that isn't the way." Clark failed in his attempt at facetiousness, but his words halted Cynthia. The slight wind drove the cold all into her heart. She couldn't see where they had come.

"It's back this way." Clark wheeled. "If you are cold —"

Without waiting for the end of his sentence, Cynthia turned and ran past him, her scarf fluttering over her shoulder. "It's warmer — running —" she panted, as she heard his feet close behind her.

"All right, come on!" She was scarcely aware that Clark thrust his arm through hers. The air stung her throat; her breath seemed to freeze before it reached her lungs. She ran and ran; where was the corner? The sidewalk began to lurch up to meet her feet. She stumbled, and Clark dragged her up.

"You're all out of breath," he gasped, but she only shook her head.

Just as her feet grew so heavy that she knew she couldn't lift them, she saw ahead the dark mass of the elm which reached up to her window, and then across the snow, patches of light from the sitting room windows. Wrenching her arm free, she whirled ahead, up the steps to the door, where, her fingers clutching the handle, she faced the boy. Stronger than her need to escape, now, was her need to send him away unwitting, to fill his eyes with dust of some untruth, that he might not see her wound.

"I — beat — you!" She shrank against the door.

"You have to pay for that!" His quick breathing burned her cheek.

Her spirit doubled and twisted like a cornered wild thing. What could she say so that he would go — would go, not knowing? His hands were on her shoulders; she pushed them off.

"No! Not any more!" she cried. "You — you'll have to run for your car. I hear it coming."

"But Cynthia — little girl!" The throaty humoring protest was close in her face.

She turned the knob, and stepped into the open door.

"You can't kiss me," she said distinctly. "I don't think it's much fun. It's rather stupid. Good night."

She closed the door and listened, in panic lest he follow her. After a moment she heard his feet, thoughtful, pausing once, and then descending the steps to the street.

She wheeled with a start as the inner door opened.

"I thought I heard you, Cynthia. What you doing here in the cold?" Her mother held the door wide. "Clark gone?"

"Yes." Cynthia clenched her hands, as though to gather all her emotions there, secure from suspicion, until she could be alone. "Yes. He had to go. I'm just taking off my things."

"Was it pretty cold?" Her mother lingered.

"Dreadfully."

"You shouldn't have gone out tonight."

Cynthia plunged desperately into the bright sitting room; there was no way to avoid the light. She was afraid to sit down there, where everything had happened last night. Her father and mother would guess!

"I think I'll go to bed," she said. The stairs beckoned to her. "I'm tired."

"Are you sick, Cynthy?" Her mother's voice came after her.

"No, not a bit." Cynthia was already halfway to the head of the stairs. "Just tired. Good-night."

She wished to lock her door, but she feared lest someone discover that she had done that and demand her reason. So she turned on the light and began to undress, thankful as many older people have been, for the reprieve of a moment through an habitual act. Her shoestring had knotted; she pulled at it with a little sob, and it broke. At length she stood by her bed buttoning her flannel nightgown. Her body felt cold as she touched it with her hand; that was strange, when waves of heat were beating in her head. She climbed slowly into bed letting herself down into the cold sheets with a shudder.

Out of the confusion of emotions that blurred and moved at the horizon of her consciousness, one emerged, expanded, grew distinct, and scorched through her. She was ashamed, ashamed. "You let me!" Clark had accused her, and she had let him. More than that, she had wished him to love her — had worse than asked him. And he had thought it fun! She would have this shame to hide all her life. She must be very sinful, a girl who liked that — she could not think the word for the caresses — when there was no love behind them. Was this the way one's heart broke? She pressed her fingers against her small breasts. She wouldn't hide her face in her arm; that would be childish — she might even cry then. This was no young sorrow, to be melted in tears. Why had she been so shameless? Through her body quivered a poignant memory, unbidden, of Clark's flushed face close to hers, of his lips. She drove the recollection away, the hot shame running up into her very eyelids.

70

"Oh, I don't love him!" she cried. In a moment of white penetration, she caught back her former attitude toward the boy; she had accepted him with a thoughtless tolerance because he was jolly, and tall, and personable. She sat up in bed, her lips moving. "Oh, I don't know why I did it!" Within her worked an inarticulate bewilderment that things without reality could seem so beautiful, could cause such emotion.

At the sound in the hall she dropped back against the pillow pulling the clothes up to her chin. As the door opened carefully she held her breath; she would pretend to sleep.

But her mother came in and sat down on the bed.

"I've brought you some hot cocoa, Cynthy," she said, and Cynthia knew she was peering anxiously through the dimness. "You'll sleep better."

Cynthia could see the swirl of steam from the cup held toward her. She didn't want it! But drinking it might be the quickest way to regain solitude. Propping herself on an elbow, she gulped recklessly choking a little as she tasted the thick sweetness. It brought tears into her eyes, but that, and the hot pain in her chest after she had swallowed, gave her a curious relief, as if she suffered in atonement for a sin. She lay down again, shrinking from her mother's hand as it touched her forehead.

"You aren't sick, Cynthia?"

"No, I said I wasn't."

"Is anything the matter?"

Cynthia's heart gave a jump, and then ran into quick beating, in her breast, in her throat, in her temples. Had her mother heard — last night? Had she guessed?

"Why, no!" she exclaimed, and then added hastily, "What made you think so?"

71

"You haven't had a quarrel with Clark?" Her mother's voice was a worried, repressed caress.

"No." Cynthia bit off her laugh suddenly; it felt as if it were about to run up into a scream. "We — we never quarrel. What would we quarrel about?"

"Well," her mother sighed. "You aren't going too far with him, are you? He isn't worth it. Your father says he's just a light-weight fellow."

"I don't know what you mean. You want me to have some fun, don't you?"

She hadn't meant to say quite that, and the phrase "some fun" was a hot wind, shrivelling her against the pillow. Remotely she heard her mother.

"Of course. But I don't want anybody to make you unhappy. You're too young for that sort of thing."

Cynthia stared at her mother's face, just visible in the streak of light from the hall lamp. "That sort of thing!" Then her mother knew — had some knowledge about things. Unconsciously Cynthia groped toward her; perhaps she would explain. Before her hand touched that of her mother, however, it dropped, checked by the old habit of inhibition. Her mother would not understand. She would say, "You are too young to think of such things."

And when the mother, a little wistfully, brushed the hair from Cynthia's forehead, and leaning over, kissed her cheek, Cynthia lay very still, struggling with a resentment which seemed disloyal, a resentment that these older people had knowledge they concealed so carefully.

Her mother rose.

"Good-night, dear. You were up too late last night, I guess. And you probably talked all the night before. Go right to sleep. I'll call you in time tomorrow."

In the doorway for an instant she paused, a rather weary silhouette; then Cynthia was alone again.

She was sleepier; the brief contact with her usual life had dulled the edge of her emotions. At any rate, no one knew. Clark didn't know; he would think she had been playing with him. And her mother didn't guess. She turned curling her arm under her head. Mary wouldn't ask her questions. She opened her eyes for a moment. Did Mary know things, she wondered, except the feeling of them? She closed her heavy eyelids. "Am I very sinful," she thought. Turning a little more, she pressed her eyes against her arm wondering dimly why the gold and blue spots danced about on her eyelids. Perhaps, if she understood more, she would become better. With a faint sigh she slept.

Helen Hull and Mabel L. Robinson as "The Bicycle Girls" in Maine, c. 1918.

DISCOVERY

"Let's sit here and talk a while." Richard stepped over the low hand rail of the bridge and sat down on the end of a plank, dangling long legs over the water, yellow with spring turmoil. Cynthia followed him, stopping to release her skirt as a nail caught it.

"Don't you wish you wore trousers?" He threw back his head, glints of orange in his gray eyes.

"Skirts are always catching you." Cynthia sat down gravely beside him. "But I don't want to be a man, if that's what you mean."

"Yes, you do! Then you could do what you please. Now you have to fall in love with somebody and marry him."

"I don't have to." Cynthia pulled at her glove, uneasy under Richard's eyes. Perhaps tan gloves weren't just the thing for Sunday, with a white waist and black skirt.

"That's the fate society gives you," he was saying lazily. She tucked the gloves under her, on the side away from Richard. "Now, I can do what I like, and then some day, when I decide it's wise, I can marry one of you, waiting for her fate."

"I might do what I like."

"That's what women like."

"I hate you when you talk like that!" She flushed at his laugh.

"Don't hate me." He put his and over hers, turning it, his fingers around her wrist. Cynthia tried to hush the stirring in her pulses before his fingers caught it. "Perhaps that isn't your fate." Her hand lay, palm up, in his. "You haven't a lady's hand, have you? You could really do things with those fingers."

"It — it is ugly." Cynthia scarcely knew what she said; the strange pain of Richard's touch seeped through her.

"Not ugly. Useful. Strong." He drew a finger tip across the palm. "And sensitive. Are you all those things?"

Cynthia drew her hands slowly away. As she closed her fingers softly in her lap, she shut in the warm magic of his touch. He flung his arms behind his head, on the railing; Cynthia followed his eyes down the little stream to its curve between yellowing willows. Peace, full of the sound of the quick muddy water beneath her, of the touch of his fingers, shut within his palm, of the nearness of his long, still body, closed around her, lifting her out of thoughts.

Richard stirred, turning his head.

"Cynthia, I'm sorry our walks are over."

She stiffened her body against a sudden panic.

"I've got to go tomorrow. I didn't expect to leave so soon, but this job's done and the firm wants me on another."

"You were going to stay the rest of the spring." How the yellow branches of the willows swayed against their black trunks! Richard's voice tore at her.

"I suppposed I could. I'm sorry, too. I didn't expect to like being here — or mind leaving."

"It isn't much of a place."

"You've been the best sort of companion."

The words dispelled the blur into which river and willows had misted. Cynthia held her eyes against his steady look. Was it pity under his gentle, probing glance? She said, quite loud. "We've had a lot of good times."

"I haven't been all bad for you, Cynthia?" He had her hand again.

This — his going — was the shadow that had lain at the rim of all the flashing days since he had come, late in the fall. She knew now that she had meant to face it before the spring ended. Here it was, thrown across her like a net. Her eyes struggled against his for a moment. Then she climbed to her feet, freeing her hand.

"How silly! What do you mean?"

Richard swung around, his eyes still searching.

"Interrupting the even tenor of your respectable ways —"

"Is that what you think you've done!" Cynthia stepped over the rail. She must escape before his eyes had probed through to her agony. We'll be late for dinner

77

now," she said, desperately, and started on a run up the muddy lane.

Richard came up with her, easily, caught her hand, and drew her into a swifter run. The ground was soft beneath their feet; the wind which lifted Cynthia's hair seemed like the green flash in the trees taken to flight. The chaos in the girl whirled up on the rhythm of their motion into a shining paean of suffering. At the end of the lane Richard vaulted the bars; Cynthia stumbled, trembling. She was back in her clumsy, halting body again, struggling for breath. Drooping there, she saw her boots, mud spattered. She had felt beautiful as she ran! Richard waited, head back, the sun on his strong throat. He could love only someone full of grace and beauty —

As they picked their way across the road to the sidewalk, Cynthia hunted for words to throw across the silence.

"Where do you go from here?"

Richard looked down at her deliberately before he answered.

"Funny, isn't it, how little we really know about each other. What we mean to do, what we are like. If I say I'm going home for a few weeks, it doesn't mean much to you, does it? And you never let me see far under your smile, do you?"

"We know some things — enough, I guess." Cynthia quickened her steps down the village street. Would he pull down the self she had built so diligently for him? She had a glimpse of the pictures she had piled on the floor of her closet: the Madonna her mother had given her, the gilt-framed group of her society at school. She had thrust them there that first night he had come to see her, for fear they might amuse him. Did he know about those and all the other things she had concealed? He was smiling now.

"What is enough?"

She fought away her shame in a laugh.

"Well — I know what you like best for dinner."

"True." He paused, and Cynthia felt his grin release the trap that had threatened. He had taught her that trick — of escaping into trivialities. "That is important. I hope the Moores know, too. I've got to dine there today. Mutual friends, etcetera. I'm sorry — the last day."

"They'll give you a better dinner than Mrs. Claude." Cynthia nodded, flushing, in return to the suspicious "How-de-do, Miss Bates," from a woman puffing past them in tight-busted black silk.

"She'll tell on you to your school board, going walking with me on Sunday morning. She is late!" Richard waved his hand toward the quiet houses. "Everyone is in the bosom of his family, engaged in the sacred rite of the Sabbath fowl."

Cynthia smiled faintly. She had a fleeting, wistful impression of herself, coming back from church to a Sunday dinner, incredibly calm. Richard burst out in a clear whistle, something they had heard at a concert last week. She remembered it, the little theme which had come back again and again, twisted, altered. Richard had pointed it out. She hadn't known music was made like that. Richard knew so many things — things she wanted. She glanced at him, striding along, breaking into his whistle with chanted words. He was going! Within her twisted a thin wire of resentment.

They came to the square white boarding house. Richard looked down at her.

"I'll come around after supper — about seven, if I may. Got to take the midnight train."

"Well — if you think you'll have time."

79

Then she escaped, up the steps, past the people talking in the parlor, to her own room. She pulled away the screen which stood in front of the dresser, and throwing aside her hat, brushed up her fair hair. On the dresser lay the letter from her mother — what was it there about Richard? She unfolded the sheet to find the sentences again.

"Mrs. C. writes me that you are running around with that Daggart man too much. I wish you would drop him. He will only make you dissatisfied with your own station in society, and he won't ever have serious intentions. He struck me queer that time when I was visiting you and he came in. There are plenty of nice boys —"

Cynthia thrust the letter back into the envelope. She looked about the small room; her hands clenched. If she sat down there, with Richard's books among the papers on the table, with the Japanese print he had brought her staring at her from the wall, with his tobacco pouch on the chair by her cot, where she had been mending it that morning — She ran out of the room.

Mrs. Claude had just come to the foot of the stairs to call her to dinner. She wore a bright blue waist; Cynthia had seen her, late the night before, hurrying to finish it. Its hard, shiny surface grayed her face. Cynthia descended slowly.

"Dinner's just ready, Cynthia." She slipped one hand into the girl's arm. "Have a pleasant walk? You missed a fine sermon." She led her across the hall to the parlor. "Now my family is all here." With her free hand she included the waiting boarders in a gesture of expansive motherliness.

Miss Murray, the music teacher, laid aside her paper with a crisp, "All but Mr. Daggart."

"He's dining with the Moores." Mrs. Claude boasted gently; none of them were likely ever to be asked to dine at that house.

In the stuffy little dining room, Cynthia bent over her plate, conscious of heat and wretchedness deferred. She was flicked into spurts of animation by the fear that they would connect her silence with Richard's absence, with his departure, when they learned of that. Between the draped lace curtains she could see the wind outside dallying in the branches of a little poplar; inside the warm odors of food weighted her eyelids.

Later, in her own room, she flung open the windows and sat down at her table. She had work to do, lots of it. These last weeks it had piled up there, neglected. She pulled a set of papers toward her, spread them open. The wind fluttered them beneath her fingers. Downstairs Miss Murray was playing. She crept to the door and opened it softly. What did she play? Something hard and flashing. Richard would be amused if he should catch her there, not knowing. She left the door ajar as she went back to her table. Perhaps — if she had known about music — After all, that was but one out of all the things. She sat, her hands folded on the papers, while the music assailed her.

At a sound she turned. Mrs. Claude stood in the doorway, her face deprecatory. She closed the door, and drawing a chair near Cynthia, settled herself.

"You aren't too busy to talk, I hope?" She nodded at the papers.

Cynthia shook her head.

"I want you to think I'm speaking as if you were my own daughter. You won't mind my speaking frankly."

Cynthia, dry-throated, lied. "Why, no."

"It's just that we are interested in you, Cynthia. You don't realize — you're too young. But folks are talking."

81

"About what?" Cynthia's eyes travelled up over the slippery blue waist, past the tight high collar, to Mrs. Claude's eyes, dark circled, above high cheek bones.

"About your Mr. Daggart. What good can come of your — well, if it was anyone else but you I'd say almost — throwing yourself at him?"

Cynthia's heart gave a great leap, and hot blood rushed into her throat. She pressed herself rigidly against her chair.

"I thought it wasn't my business until yesterday," Mrs. Claude went on, slowly. "His landlady told me about the pictures of a girl he's got his room full of. He's engaged to her."

"What difference does that make?" The hot flood receded, leaving Cynthia frozen under Mrs. Claude's curious eyes.

The woman laid her hand, a large hand with brown spots between the veins, on the girl's knee.

"I hope it don't. But you don't want to spend all your time with a man that's going to marry someone else. Hours he's here in your room" — she paused, the corners of her mouth puckering — "and the door shut!"

"We — we read together —" Cynthia's body trembled under the woman's hand.

"How many folks would believe that?"

Cynthia stared at the sallow face; in her breast a sickening whirl began.

"What harm is there in reading?" She hated herself for the faltering of her voice.

"You can't neglect what things look like to folks. I know you mean all right. I blame him. He's older, and just because you made him comfortable and he could play with you —"

82

"You needn't blame anybody." A sudden rage steadied the whirling. "I know what I've been doing. If Mr. Daggart is interesting, can't I see him? There are other things besides — whatever you mean!"

"I spoke for your own good." Mrs. Claude drew her hand away. "If you want to throw away your good name and your chances for marriage —"

"What I can lose as easily as that isn't worth much!"

"Why, Cynthia!" Mrs. Claude shook her head. "He isn't worth it. He's selfish, or he wouldn't have hung around you so, and him engaged. And he's — well, I've looked into some of his books." She pointed to those on the table. "I don't think they'll do you any good. A man who wants to bring a girl things like that!"

"There's no use talking about it." Cynthia rose and stood by the window, her arms stiff at her sides. A quivering weariness beset her; she was afraid she might cry. "It's all over. Mr. Daggart is going away tonight. His work is done."

Mrs. Claude got to her feet slowly.

"I hope you understand. I thought I ought to say something."

"Oh, I understand!" Cynthia checked herself. Mrs. Claude's lips were twitching. Cynthia stared at her, at her heavy, graceless body, flat-chested, wide-hipped; at her gray-toned face. A woman like that could tell you what to do, just how to live — to make a good marriage, to grow like her! Cynthia pressed her lips against a laugh. It was funny! Richard would think it amusing, not insulting. She relaxed.

"Yes." She began again, the sound of her own voice steadying her. "I see how you meant it. But it isn't necessary to bother any more." The color flared into her face.

Mrs. Claude ran her fingers along the seam of her sleeve.

"If you do understand —"

"Oh, I understand. It isn't what you do, is it? It's how it looks. But Mr. Daggart's going away. So there's nothing else to say."

She waited, motionless. When, a moment later, Mrs. Claude had withdrawn, incoherently, she slipped into her chair. Her finger tips prickled with a curious sense of power. What had she done? She had been frightened, terrified, when Mrs. Claude came in. Then she had climbed for an instant above herself, to a tiny peak of strength, and Mrs. Claude had crept away, silenced. Why, it had been easy, downing her.

But folks were talking, pitying her! Her body contracted with the nausea of humiliation. Richard was going — back to that other girl. He had referred to her once, casually; and Cynthia had beaten off the buzzing thought of her with blind hands, as though by forgetting she could drive the girl out of existence. Someone rich — beautiful.

She bent over the pile of school exercises. The childish writing sprawled under her eyes. Resolutely she held the sheet closer, until unwillingly her mind responded. She picked up a pencil and went methodically to work.

Hours later she leaned back in her chair, rubbing her strained eyes. Dusk had floated into the corners of the room and blurred the writing. She sorted out the sheets, laid them in a drawer, and pushed her chair away from the table. Her body ached from the rigid hours. At any moment now Richard might come in. Suppose she were to go away, not be there when he came. She vibrated under the fear that a whim of her own could banish her from that last encounter. Slipping to the floor by her cot she

84

laid her cheek on the leather pouch. The smooth odor of tobacco and old leather crept through her.

Someone called her; she stumbled to her feet and pulled open the door.

"Oh, she is in," Mrs. Claude answered. "Just go right up."

She retreated a step into the room, fumbling for the electric button. She must have been asleep; her blood rippled from the sudden awakening. The light flashed on.

"Is this the room?" It wasn't Richard's voice. Startled, she faced a tall, fair boy, thrusting a hand toward her self-consciously.

"Guess you didn't expect me." Their hands touched, and Cynthia's confusion cleared. It was Clark Walton. She felt as though she had forgotten the lines of her part, and taken a fresh start at the beginning. Still, he was following her into the room as though he did belong to the present, explaining.

"My aunt told me you were here, teaching. I'm here just over night, on my way west. Thought I'd run in — if you aren't busy."

Cynthia pushed the cushions into a pile and sat down on her couch.

"It's been a long time, hasn't it?"

"A long time —" Her cheeks were warm. In Clark's eyes she saw the counterpart of her thought. Not since that winter night when he had kissed her; she had a flicker of tolerance for that young self who had taken the kisses so seriously.

He leaned forward in his chair, rushing into a torrent of details. He was pretending not to remember. Cynthia, listening, peered at her clock. After eight! The present clutched her again. She had slept — Richard had come while she slept! What was Clark waiting for?

"Yes?" Her hand closed over the soft pouch. Richard had gone!

"So I'm going out there. Don't you think it's a good opening?"

He was taller than Richard, heavier. How sleek and plump his face looked!

"Now tell us about you. Like being the school ma'am?"

Cynthia heard his question remotely, and answered it: "That's too dull to talk about."

"Going to stay on here?"

"Stay on?" The query became a strong magnet, pulling together the scattered bits of herself. "No —" she hesitated. "No! I'm going away."

"Getting married, eh?"

"Is that all there is to do?"

"For girls, isn't it?" Clark's smile chaffed at her.

"You seem to think so." Cynthia jumped to her feet. "You wait and see." She moved to the window. "It's warm here, don't you think?" She was dizzied by the monotonous clamor within her: Richard is gone, is gone — shot through by this new, unsummoned challenge. She would go away! She could do — something! She pushed the window high and brushed aside the muslin curtain. In came the night wind, a faint smell of winter in its warmth. As she turned she found Clark staring at her, his lips parted, his eyes warm.

"You're a lot prettier than you used to be."

"Am I?" She leaned against the casement, her eyes clinging to him. Through her, a new note in the clamor sounded a faint alarm; it grew into a steady purple chanting. Clark wanted to kiss her! She had only to smile. She let her eyelids fall. Her body tingled under sudden desire — desire for lips on hers, for arms about her; it would be better than the lonely ache. Slowly she lifted her eyes. Clark had leaned forward into the strong glow from the lamp, his full lips parted; into his begging sprang a hint of certainty, of assurance. He looked silly hanging there — like a fish! Calmly she passed him to her seat on the couch, an ironic self contempt freezing the erotic tingle in her pulses. She watched him settle back, hunting for something to cover his disappointment.

"Where was it you said you were going?"

"I haven't decided yet."

He fumbled with the books at the edge of the table.

"Do you read all these? I was reading a good story the other day —" He trailed off into silence.

He had come in to see if he could kiss her again. That was all he wanted, all he thought she was for. And she had almost —

"Don't have much time for such stuff as books, now I'm working." He rose abruptly. "Have to be running on. Just stopped in for old times, you know."

Cynthia stood facing him, her eyes amused. He knew she was laughing at him! He was uncomfortable. Again the thrill of power touched her. He had no part in things that mattered. He was only a boy who had thought girls were to be kissed. She had almost slipped back into his world. Now he knew she stood outside it. What was he saying?

"Well, good night, Cynthia. Good luck to you. Glad I saw you."

"Good luck to you, too, Clark." She smiled at him, almost flauntingly. "Goodbye."

He left the door open. She heard him in the hall below, as she stood, her hands clasped, her cheeks burning. He had been a whimsical gesture to show her — but Richard had gone! She would go, too. Somewhere away from the

Clarks and Mrs. Claudes; there was a world of things to discover. She had lived, all her life, within provincial walls, meekly enough. Outside lay the world, a place of formidable beauty, not open to her. At Richard's touch the walls had crumbled. She hadn't seen that they were down, until this moment. Now she stared out across great stretches of space. What had Richard said? "Why don't you go off and see things?" And when she answered that she had no money, he had laughed. "No money? That's nothing but an excuse."

In the hall below, the door opened again; quick feet on the stairs. Before she quite understood what her heart caught in a mad leap, Richard was in the room.

"I couldn't escape earlier." He flung himself on her couch. "Behold me, a lamb rescued from the altar of convention. I'm sick of sitting up straight."

Cynthia crumpled into a chair.

"You haven't gone," she said softly. This Richard in careful dress was more terrifying than the Richard of old clothes and orange tie.

"My trunk is packed. I'm about to go. I know it's late — I won't stay. Mrs. Claude has her basilisk eye upon me from below." Back of his nonsense his eyes held her searchingly.

"Why bother to come?"

"Cynthia! I wanted to see you. Not to commit the absurdity of saying goodbye —"

"Why then?" She hugged her arms to her body. His eyes were curious. He wanted to see how she took his going!

"Cynthia —" He leaned toward her, his hand touching her knee. "You aren't going to be unhappy?"

She lifted her eyes from his strong, thin fingers to his face; under the slight pressure of his hand her body

88

relaxed. For a poignant moment she offered him her eyes, and his, dark, narrowed, sought and demanded; a pallor of submission glistened on her forehead. Then, smiling gently, he spoke again.

"I was sure you understood the situation. I didn't want to go off thinking I hadn't played square with you."

Played with her — that phrase, the assurance in his tone, his smile, wrenched Cynthia out of her lethargy.

"We've sort of drifted along, but we knew it was a charming interlude. This afternoon I heard something said about us — sort of a joke —"

"What did you hear?" Cynthia's voice was clear and still. "What is it you want now?"

"Nothing." He drew his hand away. "I haven't made you —"

"No!" Cynthia pushed her chair away impatiently, and stood, her face in the shadow. "You aren't leaving me broken hearted. You want me to tell you that you aren't to blame — I shouldn't have understood if you hadn't come back tonight — condescending —"

"Cynthia! What are you saying?"

"Just that you needn't worry about me!" How startled he looked, almost like Clark! Ah, the two were alike, except that Richard dealt in subleties. He had come back, not to kiss her, but to see her loving him, to say he was sorry.

"What's happened to you, Cynthia?" Richard plunged to his feet, followed her to the window.

"I don't know just what." She smiled and threw back her head, to meet his eyes fairly. What she saw, no longer pity nor amusement, was wind to the fires that cleansed her. "You've had a lot of fun, showing off, haven't you!"

"Cynthia, on my word, I've liked you —"

89

"Yes? But I amused you. And you thought — 'Poor little thing, how she loves me!' Only you didn't see that it wasn't just you. I found out this afternoon. It was all the things you had. The things you stood for. I wanted them and thought I couldn't have them. And so I was — humble."

She threw her shoulders back; the strong tide of her self surged up, drowning the old humilities and embarrassments.

"Cynthia, I haven't been such a cad!" Richard's voice had a raw edge.

"I didn't care." Cynthia's intensity irradiated her. "Don't you see, you had everything I wanted. So I hid away, and tried to be what I thought you'd like. It must have been — flattering."

"It was — flattering." Richard's face whitened. "And I wasn't big enough. I'm — sorry."

"No." She made a quick beseeching gesture. "Don't. It doesn't matter, now." Now that she no longer feared that tolerance in his eyes, it was gone. In its place had come recognition. Again the thrill of power rushed through her. They were facing each other in reality for the first time, and it was he who was humble!

"Whatever I've done, you're more than even, laying me out like this!" For Cynthia, the bitterness in his voice had a cool, sharp taste. "I thought you enjoyed the things we did — together."

"Oh, Richard!" Cynthia laughed. In a flash of penetration she saw his glance toward her, uncertain, eager, as the symbol of all the days since he had come and she had given him that same homage. "After all, you've helped set me free."

"I haven't helped." Richard's hands closed over both of hers. "You've done it."

90

"You know it's true, then?"

Richard held her hands against his cheeks for a moment.

"True? You make me afraid of you." He spoke abruptly. "What are you going to do?"

Cynthia looked about the little room. The confusion from Richard's touch was gone, in a strong, passionless light.

"I will find out. I am going away. I am going ahead for what I want, as you do!"

"It's been there, in you. That's why —" He stood close to her. "And I must go off — to watch you from some corner?"

"Well, you were going!" Cynthia smiled.

"You don't hate me?"

"I'm grateful to you." Laying her hands on his shoulders, Cynthia drew herself up to his lips, and kissed him, gravely. "There. Now — Goodbye."

He crossed the room, reluctantly. At the door he turned, with a slight gesture of farewell.

"I don't want to go."

Cynthia smiled again. The smile deepened when, still at her window, she heard his slow steps down the quiet night street.

Helen Hull at her house in N. Brooklin, Maine, c. 1918.

THE FUSING

"Game!" Cynthia's plunging stroke had carried her to the edge of the court. She dropped to the grass. "My set, too!" she called.

The man rounded the net posts and looked down at her, flicking his racket against his neat gray trousers.

"You must have known how to play and let me think I was teaching you."

"No. But you see, I had you as a teacher." Cynthia smiled at the quick preening of his ruffled vanity.

"I'll beat you yet!"

The threat was open, in the quick flicker of his lips, in the nervous hand he thrust through his heavy, grayish hair. Cynthia stared at him: the game had left no trace of dishevelment or warmth on his lean face and body.

"Help me up." She held out her hand. "They want the court."

He drew her to her feet, releasing her fingers with a quick pressure.

"We're through," she called, to two boys in flannels. "Pretty work, isn't it!" She watched the swift volleying for a moment before she turned to cross the campus.

The late afternoon sun stretched blue shadows of the Gothic buildings across the grass; except for the white, sunken courts and the darting figures on them, a massive quiet lay in the gray walls and their shadows. Cynthia flung up her head into the breeze from the lake.

"It's almost over, isn't it? The summer." Mr. Preston jerked his words at her with a motion of his head. "You'll be going back to work."

"I don't know what I'm going to do. It seems as though this must last forever." She smiled under his doubtful glance. He wanted to take that personally! "Don't bother to come to the house with me."

"Where are you going to have dinner?"

"I don't know."

"Come back to the Commons."

That persuasive male note! He thought she was being coy. His face had a little grimace of cajolery.

"We haven't many more nights, Miss Bates. The lake will be very nice tonight — and I'd like to see you."

"I have work to do."

"What? Another of your little stories?" Strife between them again, the flare in his eyes heightening the glow in Cynthia's body. He touched her arm. "Come back. I'll wait for you there."

"Don't wait." She was off, swiftly.

As she ran up the stairs of the apartment where she roomed, the frown between her fine brows disappeared, and she laughed. She stripped off her clothes, and flinging on a kimono, ran down the hall to the bathroom. Under the shower she stretched herself radiantly to the stinging water. How good her body felt, firm, slender!

Back in her room she dressed slowly. Her cool skin, the enclosing touch of fresh garments, the strong, slow rhythm of her heart, the little breeze seeking her through the curtains — those things ensphered her; and all about her, thoughts of the evening, of the man, of her work, tugged at their leashes.

At a knock on her door she emerged reluctantly from her mood.

"Oh, Mona! Hello."

Mona closed the door and came close to Cynthia, just touching her bare shoulder with soft fingers.

"Cyn — I'm grateful to you." Her white eyelids quivered.

"You may well be! But your young man isn't." She gave Mona a push toward the couch. "Sit down while I dress." She drew her dress over her head, adding as she shook its white folds into place, "if he hadn't been a gentleman, he would have dragged me out by the scruff of my neck."

"Oh, he's too good."

Cynthia found her mood of excitement flowing back, with Mona part of it.

95

"Why do you do it?" she demanded.

"What?"

"Play with him. Let him think you'll marry him." Cynthia's cheeks warmed to her own ruthlessness. "If you hadn't looked so terrified last night, I never should have stayed."

"I had to have a buffer, Cyn."

"Throw him over!"

Mona shook her head.

"I'll marry him next month."

"When you won't even let him kiss you after he comes a hundred miles —"

"I'm not married — yet."

Cynthia bent over her, pursuingly.

"Why do you go on?"

"Oh, you with your why's! Don't you see, I'm not clever like you. I'm just — pretty. So I get married as well as I can."

"Why to that man? What about Rush?" In Mona's eyes, before she lowered her lids, Cynthia saw the leap of something like the strife in her own blood.

"I hate Rush." Mona's voice was sleepy. "Hate him. Andrew — will make a splendid husband, Cyn dear. I can manage him."

"He's too decent to be played with."

"Well, I'm going to marry him." Mona leaned forward. "Known him since childhood. Always meant to end up with him. Now you've scolded enough." She made a plunge at Cynthia and clung to her, so that Cynthia felt the tremble of her body. "What are you doing yourself with that gray gentleman?" She cupped Cynthia's cheek in a warm palm, with a "better hurry. You'll be too late to meet him."

"Then I shouldn't have to decide what I want to do."
Cynthia released herself and turned to the small mirror.
"Yes, white is good on you." Mona backed toward the
door. "Subtly alluring. What else could you want, Cyn?"
"I want to stay here and work. Can you imagine
that?"
"No, you don't! You want what we all want — a man
fooling along —" Mona blew her a kiss as she closed the
door.

Cynthia stood by her table, laying her hand on the
scattered sheets of paper. They troubled her; they almost
reached her, pulling — then they were dead and white,
and she ran out of the room.

Mona's words played across the pattern of her
thoughts as she walked the few blocks to the Commons.
Were they true? She hadn't meant to go back. Scorn
rippled through her, but she went on into the dusky,
vaulted hall, and became one of the line winding,
tray-laden, under the great Gothic arches, past the
refectory tables, past the small windows where food was
thrust at you. She liked dining there, with the somber hall
subduing the little noises of rattling china, the small
odors of food, the movement of men and women.

She carried her tray to the end of the hall, where she
could watch the other tables as she ate. There was no one
near her whom she knew, although the faces were half
familiar, like the unnoticed design of old wallpaper. Then
she saw Mr. Preston, sidling toward the door, laughing at
a jest of the stocky man beside him. She bent over her
plate, smiling. Was he afraid he might compromise
himself by eating with her, or only afraid he might have to
pay for her dinner? She wasn't hungry, but for a long time
she sat there, dallying.

What was he really like, that man? She had met him the first week at the University, had accepted him as a scholar, a man to admire. All the glamour of the University had clothed him. She remembered the strange ecstasy that had held her that first night; she had sat alone at dinner, under these arches, and from the lift of the dark timbers, the movement of strange bodies beneath them had entered into her the assurance of the miracle at last. She had struggled so long, so incredibly to make the coming possible. Surely here she could find the miracle of fulfillment. She had flung herself out of her old life into this, expecting it to pick her up with wise hands, to give her, somehow, satisfying direction for the troubled strivings within her. Then, bit by bit, she had lost the ecstasy. The University, which had been a vague and beautiful idea, splintered into a thousand particles — classes in hot and dusty rooms, people picking busily at facts — all remote, leaving her quite unchanged. There remained this man, always at her shoulder, now. She still hoped she might find reason for his presence there, some mark which distinguished him from other men.

Finally she loitered to the door, out into the bright twilight. At the end of the street a strip of lake clung to the sky.

Abruptly he was beside her, his heavy eyebrows lifted drolly.

"Tennis must have made you hungry."

"I supposed you would have gone."

"Oh, you did!" He laughed and they walked on together. "I thought you couldn't really stay in such a night, working on your little —"

"If you call them little stories again, I'll go and work!"

"Just a joke. I'm sure they're very nice."

"You aren't sure of anything about them." Cynthia met his smile with sharp hostility.

"I know you take them seriously."

"No one else does — yet." Cynthia's eyes held the widening blue of the lake. "Some day you'll have to take them as I do." The words rose within her, like slow bubbles breaking at the surface of a deep pool, from some living thing, hidden in the depths.

They went in silence through the clattering gloom under the elevated tracks. As they came out, Cynthia turned wistfully. Perhaps he might listen, if she should try to tell him. He tucked a hand under her elbow and swung her off the road into a path across the green of the park.

"Too many folks down that way." His slow smile tingled through Cynthia, and swiftly as a sea-thing contracts, her mood closed into a derisive shell.

"I feel like celebrating." He moved closer to her. "Cleared a pile today off a real estate deal. Didn't know I was a good hand at business, did you!"

There was significance in his words; Cynthia caught that in the flare of his nostrils, in the busy glancing of his eyes.

"I don't know anything about you!" she cried. "Why are you here, studying? You don't care about it —"

"Well —" He stared at her cautiously. "I do care, in a way." His face twisted into rapaciousness. "I mean to be somebody! I might have done it in business. There's a sort of prestige, though — I want that." He laughed, uneasily. "I wouldn't tell that to many."

Cynthia pressed her lips against a laugh. That was his secret desire! But fear streaked her derision, as though in his confession lay a claim upon her.

99

They stood beside the shore drive, while a string of automobiles passed. Once across they were at the lake, their feet slipping in the sand. The breeze had gone and with it the bright color, but the smooth, darkening water gave off an odor, cool, wet. The silence in which they walked had a disturbing pulse. They came to the long wooden pier.

"Let's go out there. It's cooler —" His fingers shut about her arm.

Beneath them came the muffled tones of water against the piles. Cynthia felt that they followed the twilight as it slipped from the land out over the surface of the water. When they reached the end of the pier, she looked back. Only a curve of raying lights marked the dark shore, although a glow still moved on the water. That, too, would go presently.

She sat down, leaning against a huge pile. Behind her Mr. Preston stood, tapping his fingers on the log. The sound and the slap of water below her made a tiny syncopated rhythm of suspense. The tapping ceased; the fingers touched her throat. Cynthia lifted her face, and suddenly the man slipped down beside her, his arm about her shoulders, his lips eager on her mouth. Through her something great, soft, dark, like the night, rose to her lips, held her there a long, unresisting moment. She put up her hand and pushed away the strange face. But the man kissed her fingers and brushed them away. Cynthia, eyes closed, felt his lips move from her throat, up, up to her lips, and again that great, dark presence crowded out herself. When he let her go, struggling for breath, she drooped back against the pile and opened her eyes, to find that the night had dropped about them, blurring his face.

This was what she had wished! As she swung back into herself, scornfully she felt the old antagonism leap within her.

"Why do you kiss me?"

"Why?" He leaned toward her, uneasily. But she pulled herself to her feet.

"You don't love me — you just want —"

"I want you to come back here." His hand reached along the pier to her foot.

"Come back to be kissed?" That hard bright voice came from the scornful self within her in a struggle against the sweet tide that rushed up.

With a twist of his body the man was near her, on his feet.

"Want me to come after you, eh?"

Anger flared at his words. But he laid his hands on her shoulders, and the next instant she had become again part of the summer night with its rhythmic sound of water.

Finally she pushed herself away from him, feeling the great beating of his heart under her fingers.

"Don't go — not yet!" He caught at her arm. "Stay — longer —"

His whisper, vibrating with secrecy, tore through Cynthia like the rending of fabric. Far to the south of them a broad tongue of flame from a furnace leapt into the dark sky, hung a moment, and fell. The whisper, close to the girl's ear — "Come" — drove her suddenly back along the pier.

Not until they reached the glow under the lamp on the shore did Cynthia look at the man. He blinked at her with a smile under which she winced. They went slowly along a gravel path.

"You know, we get on famously, I think." He hugged her arm. "Lots better than I thought we would —"

"Get on!" His complacency shivered down through Cynthia's murkiness.

"Well, we seem to hit it off, eh? And I've been thinking —" He spoke jerkily, like one who tries a road into a swamp, balancing backward as he advances — "I'm most through the grind here. A man gets tired of furnished rooms, being alone — you know. I pick up enough money on the side. Next year I can land a good job, with my degree. You — you're all right. A little offish, but I like it. Why not try it out?"

"Marry you?" Cynthia thrust her question straight into his maze.

"Why, yes. Two healthy, normal people —"

"But I don't love you —"

They had come to a bridge across the lagoon. Cynthia rested her arms on the rail and watched the water quiver through the band of light spilled from a lamp on the bank. The shadow of the bank, the light, held a poignant warning which scattered at the touch of the man's fingers on her arm, hot, insinuating, through the thin silk of her sleeve.

"Love?" He brought his fist down on the rail. "I swore I'd never let a woman make a fool of me again. One did, once." His voice thickened. "But you're straight enough." "His fingers moved in the hollow of her elbow. "We could go away for September, honeymooning."

His touch and his words whirled together through her; his touch drawing her to the deep, soft gulf where she lost herself; his words stirring a bright hard core to ridicule, disdain.

His arms slipped around her waist; his words ceased. But at footsteps behind them on the bridge he released her so quickly that her passivity dropped away in a laugh. Oh, but he was wary!

She walked on. He followed, peering at her face.

"Think it over. I don't mind saying I hadn't expected to take to you —"

The angle of his head had caution tinged with curiosity. Until this moment Cynthia had never thought of him as permanent in her life. Into her mind drifted impersonal phrases: a good offer, marry and settle down. She didn't know where they came from; bits of cobweb that clung to her. Was this what she wanted? He stripped himself of all glamor, and still — She laughed.

"Why, I don't even know your first name!"

"You don't?" He objected, sulkily, to her frivolousness. "Charles. Charles F. Preston."

They came in silence to the apartment entrance. In the hall, Cynthia faced him. He pulled off his hat and ran his fingers through his hair. Earlier she had thought that gesture intellectual!

"Well!" He was irritable because he was uncertain of her.

"Well?" she mocked him.

"Is there any other man?"

"Not now."

He seized her hand, but she wrenched away.

"Oh —" He humored her whim. "I'll come back tomorrow, then. About four? I can't come earlier."

Cynthia, climbing the stairs, heard the door close. She stopped.

The door of the apartment was ajar. She pushed it open. Just inside the sitting room stood Mona and Rush.

Mona swayed away from him, drooping against his arm, her eyes closed, her face a luminous mask.

Cynthia shut the door of her own room softly and in the darkness pressed her fingers on her eyes, against the image of Mona's face. It wasn't Mona's face; it was the face of a possessing emotion. At the thought, quick red shame dropped over her.

She sat down by her desk. Perhaps this was love. People — poets — wound it with beauty so that you expected more. When you really came to it, you found it just a whirl of your senses. Suppose she put this away from her and never found anything better? Charles Preston, with his thin smile. Was he the answer to her driving search?

What was he, after all? The secret strife between them had made the days interesting. A heady sauce poured over meager fare? She laid her fingers on her lips and, with a long tremble, dropped her head into the curve of her arm.

His face — so close she could discern it even in the dusk, staring, deliberate — she had closed her eyes to escape it. But she had wanted him to kiss her! Mona had said: "Well, you have to let them kiss you to see which of them you could stand marrying!"

Stand marrying! Funny, to think of it that way. Cynthia straightened her body impatiently. She must think it out, not moon about it.

Her family would be relieved to have her settle down. Settle down! Her fingers shut into her palms. That terrible eagerness which had catapulted her through objections and difficulties had left her sprawling here! She snapped on her table light and stared into the glare until black spots moved across her eyes. Perhaps Mona had been right, and she only pretended to herself. She looked down at the sheets of paper under her hands. Across them moved black specks, climbing to the edge of her circle of vision. She had worked! What did it amount to? The black specks dimmed and her eyes focused on the words she had left there.

Her little stories! Suppose she never wrote another word. Did it matter? Hundreds like her, everywhere, scribbling. Why should she take herself so seriously? Kissing — she sighed — was easier than writing. It gave you what you wanted sooner, more surely. Why not take that — and let all this striving go?

The thought was a gust bursting open the doors of her inner life, so that all the lights there twisted, swirled, like candle flames in wind. Could she live with those lights dead? Strange lights— a burrowing curiosity, rebellious, desire for the pain of giving form to things felt, seen, thought; and one leaping, erratic flame, tormenting, an urge toward power. What had these fires to do with the other self, the strong vibrant body which had gone down to the lake in quest of love?

Was it love, that dark possession? A thing which made that cleavage of desires? If there were only someone, wise, serene, who could draw this tangle through her hands and straighten it!

Cynthia pulled herself up sharply. She needn't be a silly child, at all events.

It was late. How sleep, with foment in her blood? Carelessly she gathered the scattered sheets and leaned forward, chin propped in one hand, to read what she had written. As she read, her muscles tautened; from the pages rose a sort of ghost of the living presence she had tried to set down there, a pale, dim image. On one page the ghost deepened to reality. The phrases there were almost strange to her. Had she thought them, herself? When she laid aside the last sheet, unfinished, a fierce trembling seized her, and she reached for fresh paper. She knew now what she wished to make there. It marched through her, like northern lights in a clear cold night, climbing, mounting steadily, growing in brilliance. The difficult slow period of growth was past. The story had matured in triumph.

She worked steadily, not rapidly, stopping at times to ease the cramped fingers of her hand. A white austerity hardened the lines of her brow and mouth.

She reached the end, folded the sheets. It was done, it was good; it had drained her so that she crept across to the couch and slept almost as she stretched her stiff body there.

She woke at the sound of a door slamming. For an instant she lay inert, suspended above actual consciousness. She saw the golden loop of wire in the globe of the lamp; it had burned all night. As she snapped it off, she laid her hand on the sheets of paper. Was it, after all, good? She didn't dare look at it yet. She wasn't even tired! A bath, fresh clothes, breakfast. She was starved. She pulled aside her curtains. The stretch of midway rippled under the sun in waves of golden green. The day itself was like that, stretched ahead in waves of excitement.

Later, on the stairs she met Mona, dragging heavy feet, gazing at her out of somber eyes.

"Had breakfast? Come with me." She drew Mona's hand into the crook of her arm, and led her back to the glow of the street.

The tea room was an empty checkerboard, its tables white in the sunlight. A tall boy, his hair black and stiff above his white waiter's coat, came toward them. Cynthia, detached, watched Mona's little smile, saw her glance and rich, low voice make an intimate thing out of muffins and coffee.

"You shoot it out like a — squid, don't you?" she said, as Mona, with the disappearance of the boy, settled back again into somberness. "Only it's an aura — an aura of your feminineness, whenever a man's in sight."

"He's a nice boy. Freshman. He'll bring us the best muffins he's got."

"You don't do it for muffins!"

"It's our game," interrupted Mona, sharply.

Cynthia smiled. Mona didn't want names given the game. The waiter came in with the breakfast tray.

"Is there anything else?" He glanced at Mona, deference rushing crimson into his thin face. "I have a class now —"

"Nothing, thank you."

Cynthia breathed the swirling fragrance of the coffee.

"You aren't eating a thing, Mona," she said, presently.

"I said goodbye to Rush last night." Mona stopped pushing the yellow crumbs around her plate and looked up, her eyes black in her small, white face.

"Oh — was that goodbye!"

"And I wrote Andrew that if he wanted to marry me, he had to do it now. I'm going home today."

Cynthia set down her cup.

"I've gone too far with Rush." Around Mona's lips came a white circle. "I've got to run."

"Mona!" Cynthia flung her arm across the table, touching Mona's fingers. "Why run, if you love him?"

"Love!" Mona's laugh clinked. "I can't marry him. He's a devil. A month from now I'll hate him."

"But Andrew — don't go back to him —"

"I've got to be rid of this madness. I'm marrying — safety."

Cynthia drew back in her chair.

"Well — shall I marry Preston?"

The tragedy in Mona's face shivered into a shrewd glance.

"Caught him?"

"He asked me, last night." An unexpected tide of color washed Cynthia's face.

"Did you like it?"

Cynthia's color deepened indignantly, but as her glance met Mona's mock solemn stare, it struck off a flare of laughter from the two girls, shattering the dull moment.

"Aren't we the sillies!" She leaned toward Mona again. "As if we couldn't do what we want to!"

"It isn't so simple as that." Mona's laugh died. "What one wants is — a sensation, perhaps. But we marry — for a life job. I want to be rid of myself, I tell you."

The proprietress thrust an inquiring head through the door, and Mona pushed back her chair.

"My treat! Call it a wedding breakfast."

On the steps Cynthia turned to her.

"Walk over to the library with me?" In the bright light she saw fine lines puckering the corners of Mona's eyes. She was suffering!

"Just to the corner. I'm going this noon."

"Have you packed? Can I help you?"

"I did it all last night." Mona's lips curled into an impish smile. "I was afraid I'd change my mind." After a moment, "What were you doing last night? I saw your light."

"Working. Finished a story."

"After a love scene!" Mona slipped her arm through Cynthia's. "Aren't you the queer duck! I don't believe old Preston is good enough. Don't hurry. You may find someone better."

"I'm not worried about that." They reached the corner and stopped under a great elm. Cynthia rubbed a finger against the rough bark. "What do you do," she said, slowly, "if you don't like a man — what do you do with the part of you that wants — love making?"

She could see tiny reflections of herself in Mona's dilated pupils; she held her breath. Another moment, and she would be at the center of the person behind the eyes, would know her, would disclose herself. Then, like a breeze on water, something clouded them, and Mona turned away with a shrug.

"You never admit you have it!" After an instant of closing silence, Mona pulled Cynthia's face down to hers, kissed her and backed away.

"Write to me sometime, will you? Goodbye." Her heels tapped lightly along the walk as she went.

Cynthia felt hot tears under her eyelids. They were gone when she reached the campus. She looked at the square towers lifting against the brilliant sky. They still held for her at times all the stirring possibility she had sought that summer and failed to find in the routine of work.

She walked slowly across the campus, the warm sunlight enclosing her, vibrant, expectant. She came to a pool of shade in the angle of one of the buildings, and with a sigh let herself down, a relaxed heap, on the grass. She sat quite motionless, her body curving, her hands clasped about one knee. Slowly, as though her fingers moved in dark water among strange shapes, she hunted, hunted. There was something she must find. If she waited, still, she might touch it. Then, stealthily, she had it. Fear. She had been afraid to stand out, alone, herself. Afraid to throw herself into future days. The thing was out now, in the light. Her fingers twisted about her knees. She had wished for obliteration, for a slipping down into warm darkness, with all need for struggle, for work, taken from her. The arch of her body lifted, grew proud, defiant; the thrill of the night, of the work she had done, lay upon her again, beat upon her with great wings. She pushed herself up from the ground, the sun warm on her shoulders. People were coming out of the buildings, moving across the quadrangles. She knew that there, too, she had wanted something, her vague dream of the University — something outside to hold her, cradle her. Now that she had pulled her fear, her weakness, out into the light, she could fight it.

She had no surprise when she saw Charles Preston, with his sidling, busy gait, coming toward her. He crossed the grass, stood near her.

"Good morning," he said appraisingly. "I didn't expect to see you —"

"It's just as well." Her voice was quiet. "I wanted to tell you — last night was all a mistake."

"Oh, I say!" The sun was cruel to his anger; it made him blink a little, pointed out old, hard lines in his face.

Cynthia looked at him steadily. Between them lay the tremendous distance of her discovered self, and with that a sharp, wondering consciousness of him.

110

"I'm sorry, if it matters to you — very much. But it won't."

Abruptly she left him, and went swiftly across the grass, out to the street. She had at last made a beginning of freedom — to find real love — to struggle, to work.

Helen R. Hull, 1939.

LAST SEPTEMBER

Perhaps to understand the story, you need to understand the setting. Certainly it contained, in concrete and tangible shape, the forces which worked to produce the beginning of the story. And without this particular setting, there never could have been this ending. Perhaps the extraordinary, sweet, concentrated air which runs under the great dark wings of a hurricane is in part responsible for the ending; at the very heart of darkness and destruction is this breath of concentrated life, burning out too rapidly sluggish blood, toxins of habit and hate and age. It is exhilarating as any great fear may be, it gives a kind of intoxication unlike the ordinary earthly forms in that the feeling of release, of freedom and power, is not an illusion. It may be temporary, but it is real while it lasts. And one good whiff may well make a man believe, as it penetrates to cells which had never breathed before, that the trouble with this world may be that it is keyed down to thin, dull air.

All that is surmise, but the setting itself is real enough. Some changes occurred on that day in late September, but up to that day not much had changed for more than a hundred years. A town in southern New England, touching the coast and stretching inland a few miles; the town itself centered about the river, before it spread out to make the head of the bay, bridges with turntables and draws for the vessels that came up to the docks, with warehouses and ships' chandlers' shops along the docks, with business streets, a few, at the foot of the hills, and residence streets climbing the hills; with a mill or two, and factories farther inland, along the river banks. North of the town lay farming country, and south of it the widening bay and ocean. Out of the town ran the shore road, and here macadam had replaced the original road where white sand poured from the turning rims of wheels; some of the estates had been cut into building lots for summer cottages; the tip of the western side of the bay was Grady's Amusement Park, with bathing pavilions, a skating rink, a Ferris wheel, and concession stands around the parking place for the cars which had produced this development.

A few miles out from town, where the shore thrust a finger into the bay, so that you had the last of the river on one side and what seemed to be real ocean on the other, stood the old Lathrop place. The shore drive cuts across the base of the finger, ceasing to be a shore drive for several miles. When the drive was put through, there had been some dickering through an agent with Mrs. Susan Lathrop Field, the last of the Lathrops, who was abroad at the time, in London, on the Riviera, in Cairo. She had no sentiment against selling the shore land for the drive; on the contrary, she had a desire to make good money (which she no doubt needed!) at the town's expense. Finally the town council overrode the one elderly alderman who still felt that the town owed a great deal to the Lathrop family, and voted to confiscate a right of way in a convenient straight line across the property, behind the barns and stables, and through what had been a small training track old Lathrop had used for his horses. People whizzing past in cars saw only the weathering out-buildings. In the winter the square bulk of the house showed through arching branches of the great elms and oaks, with dark rust stains from hinges of the closed shutters staining the dingy clapboards, and the two great chimneys, one at each end, standing like patient lifted ears.

Across from the barns and sheds, and in its season, the house, lay the rest of the bisected property, fields and woods, and what had originally been the farmer's house, a sturdy, story-and-a-half building, like those you see in Maine and New Hampshire. It stood on a swelling mound of land, a neat road winding past it to the garage, its paint smooth-white, its opened shutters sleek and green, the meadow tamed into a lawn under its charmingly curtained windows. *They* said that Mrs. Field had had to come down in her price, when there was no shore land left except that around the old ark that no one wanted, and almost no one remembered that Margaret Turner's father had been the farmer on the Lathrop place. For Margaret had bought the little house, and she was there, that fall of nineteen hundred and thirty-eight.

She had spent her summer holidays there even before she bought the house, and although she had never lied outright about the matter, she had somehow created for her occasional guest the impression that these were ancestral acres about her, their original glory damaged by the wanton stroke of the road through them, by the change in the quality of the residents along the western shore of the bay. Margaret had not set about creating this impression. She had said, and it was true, "When my father set out those trees," and, "Once the lawns ran to the very edge of the beach, you can't imagine how beautiful it was then!" and, "It would have broken my father's heart if he had seen what changes —" Her guests, a girl from the private school where Margaret taught mathematics, motoring with her mother to their summer place on the Cape, or two or three of her fellow teachers, skipping about the country in a polished Ford, stopped on their journey to have tea in Margaret's charming living room, with its English chintzes, hooked rugs, pieces of old mahogany and pine. As they drove away, the girl's mother might say, "You can tell that Miss Turner comes from a good family, I'm glad there's someone like that in your school," and the girl might answer, "Well, I sort of like her, although most of the girls are just paralyzed! She's terribly sarcastic." And the teachers, some of the younger members of the faculty, who had stopped to boast about their trip around the Gaspé, would say, "Of course, if you had a place like that, that had been in your family for generations, you would rather spend your summer that way. She didn't seem the least bit stuck up or cold, did she, when you see her in her own setting?" And when Margaret sighed as she said, "It would cost too much to put the big house in shape, or to run it," she was sighing in all sincerity at a dream of her young girlhood; she didn't intend to suggest a picture of herself as brave and wise, settling into the cottage, earning the money for its shingles and paint and a part-time handyman and gardener, never complaining at lost elegance and leisure.

Probably Margaret Turner never examined too closely the impression she had established about herself and the old Lathrop place. It mattered little to anyone except herself, and for herself it was like a warm, dark cloak within the folds of which she could hide the emptiness of her hands or her heart, a cloak drawn around a self not quite symmetrical nor firmly fleshed, a trifle warped and withered from meager fare, from thwartings and overstrain. She hadn't planned to weave a complete garment, she had just sketched a line or two of it, she wasn't entirely to blame if in mild gossip, casual references, people clothed her thus.

Among the items which no one except Margaret knew were these: she had spent every cent of her savings (they weren't much, on her small salary) including her one insurance policy which had matured when she was sixty, in buying the house and furnishing it; there was still a small mortgage, which she meant to pay off before she retired. She understood vaguely that the school at which she taught did something for its teachers when they were too old to be of further use. Surely enough to live on — taxes, coal, a little food. But after 1929 there had been uneasiness among the older teachers. The endowment of the school was small, the contributions from alumnae diminished (married women couldn't expect their husbands to do much for their wives' old school, not with the market the way it was!) and in the need to reduce expenses, there began a weeding out among the older

117

members of the staff. Margaret Turner held her wiry figure more erect, had her white hair waved more often, tried a little rouge under her handsome dark eyes, and moved with an effect of great vivacity about her work. "You have your own home," some of them said to her, "you don't have to worry. Did you hear about poor old Simmsy? The trustees cut her pension in half the other day, they don't know how long they can continue that pittance, Simmsy isn't seventy yet and she says all her folks live to be ninety at least."

The trustees were sorry, but there was nothing in the bond about pensions. In prosperous times they could make generous gestures, but after all, women of intelligence, on regular salaries all those years, should have some foresight about the future, and since retrenchment was necessary, it was only fair to keep the younger teachers at work. There had been a dinner last May, a dinner of farewell to two women who had been longest with the school. They weren't older than Margaret, but their age was on the record because they had started early, and had been less canny than Margaret. They'd let themselves go a little, too, Margaret thought, as she sat at the dinner listening to pleasant speeches from old girls about how much these women had meant to them. Earmarked as elderly, too comfortable about figure and dress. If she was careful, she might fool them into keeping her on for a few more years. After the dinner, in the teachers' cloak room, one of them, puffing as she bent to pull on her galoshes, said: "You know, horses have a better deal. They shoot 'em when they're through with 'em." The other, who was plump and pink and whose good humor was not yet entirely deflated by the sharp pricking point of fear, said, "There's one thing sure, we'll

118

have good company at the poorhouse. All the best people will be there!"

"Haven't you relatives?" Margaret had asked. "You used to talk about your sister's children —"

"Distant relatives." She chuckled. "That's a good phrase. Very distant. You know, in hard times there's nothing so distant as a relative. Self-protection, in case you wanted something. Don't be funny. No, the only useful relatives are the kind you have, nice ones who've passed on and left you well fixed."

She'd like to visit me this summer, thought Margaret; she saw the notion in the change it made as it crossed the woman's mind. Nothing so harsh as calculation, more a quick child-wish, as if she pressed her face, eyes round, mouth pursed a little, close to a windowpane beyond which was something longed for. I couldn't, thought Margaret; I couldn't stand having anyone around all the time, I don't really know her, anyway I couldn't afford it, I've got to be careful. "Drop in, if you're in my neighborhood." That was it, turn away quickly, you haven't seen the entreaty. "I'd be delighted to give you a cup of tea."

"Well, I don't know just where —" The porter had knocked on the door then. Mrs. Montagu, one of the old girls, was waiting; she had her car, she'd be glad to drive them home, it was raining. Margaret had bade them good night, good-by, she wasn't quite ready to go. She wasn't ready to be one of the elderly, discarded figures, with Mrs. Montagu, no doubt, feeling a pleasant glow at her thoughtful kindness to them.

The first of June, Margaret had packed her trunk, and filled a box with books and pictures, emptying the room in the residence hotel for women of every sign of her tenancy. Usually she stored the box in the basement until

119

fall, but this year she sent it by express to her house at the shore. No one noticed; there was a new management, and the chipper desk clerk didn't realize that Miss Turner had lived in the hotel since it opened. He didn't even ask if she wished the same room in the fall. At least, thought Margaret, she wouldn't regret leaving; the building had run down. And she didn't have to explain that she meant to look for a cheaper room, one where she could prepare her own breakfast, and perhaps supper. The lunches served at the school were really dinners. If she could save a little more, if she could count on two more years — if only they didn't pare the salaries another ten percent —

She spent June setting her house in order, waxing each piece of furniture, watching the warm color, the subtle texture of wood shine out as the bluish film of wax disappeared under her slow patient rubbing, polishing the silver, cleaning the rugs. She no longer did much with gardens, except for weeding around the few perennials. When she stooped over, black spots moved crazily across her eyes, and the hollows in her temples throbbed. For a few years after she bought the place, she had hired a man to help her, but fifty cents an hour was much more than she needed for her own living. She had a boy from the village come once a week to cut the grass, and on pleasant days she attacked with clippers the tufts he had left along the edge of the walk and drive, around the trees, close to the granite blocks that made the foundation of the house. In the long June evenings she crossed the highway, looking carefully in each direction to make sure no car was about to rush at her, with young voices shrieking or horns screaming; she walked past the old Lathrop house, looking up at the discolored shutters, she looked under the pines for lilies of the valley, she had picked them there when she was a child, they still grew, small sheaths of

120

green enclosing the staff of tiny, cream bells. She kicked her toe against the unkempt grass which thrust itself through the old graveled path, she frowned at the lilac bushes with the straggle of dead branches at the center, with a few brownish spikes among the heart-shaped leaves where blossoms had grown neglected in May. It just shows, she said. It just shows! They had everything to start with, everything, and I had nothing. Now Susan Lathrop is a ruined old woman with no one to say a good word for her, and I — her face set in bleak pride — no one has ever had a word to breathe against me. No hint of the slightest scandal. Although it wasn't easy, always —

The grounds in front of the house looked green in the soft twilight, with the pointed blades of June grass, but as she crossed them, her feet sank into the matted grayish tangle of old, uncut growth. As Margaret went toward the shore she thought, I'd like to see Susan Lathrop face to face, I'd like to ask her — I'd say, how could you do this to yourself, how could you fall so far? Look at the two of us now, think what you had then, money, beauty, position, safety, love, oh, most of all, love! Because of you my brother ran away, and died. He was going to make a fortune for you in the copper mines, you couldn't wait! And Lester Field had begun to love me, when you came home that summer. I was nobody, and you — you were Susan Lathrop. And now, people respect me! But they snicker when they speak your name.

Sometime, surely, they would meet, and Margaret would speak out. She could scarcely have bought her house for this one purpose, she could not have said why she had such satisfaction in the small perfection of her own place and the steady disintegration of the large house and its grounds, but as she thought of Susan she drew in her full upper lip so that her mouth was thin and hard,

121

and her eyes, under the deep arched lids, were black-brown, pupil and iris merged in hatred. When she reached the edge of the land, she would shake herself, thrusting her hands into the pockets of the leather jacket she wore against the evening air, she would say, why do I bother with thoughts of her, here's this nice sea air to breathe, and even a little sunset left. Sometimes she sat on the rickety steps of the old bath-house, watching the flat sand run with opalescence as the tide came slowly, spreading the curving edge of thin advancing water, withdrawing it, in rhythm which seemed so hesitant that she was astonished when at last there was water at her feet. The tide eddied in lines of color about the irregular dark piles which marked the line of the long pier; the pier itself had cracked up in winter ice, had been carried away piece by piece. Beyond the tip of land the water of the outer bay was already darker, its movement shaking off the reflection of lingering sunset color. Sometimes Margaret walked through the stiff grass to the outer shore, but not often; the rocks there scuffed her shoes, the air was colder, and well down the bay the lights of the amusement park twinkled crazily, like a dissipated, earthbound constellation. Always when she turned away from the water she was surprised to find the land so dark, evening already caught around the old house, under the trees. She would walk more quickly, feeling dew from the long grass on her ankles, looking to right and left before she crossed the highway, and sometimes as she waited, while a car roared past, the glare of the headlights briefly on the great barn, on a bit of broken paddock fence, she could see, before the thicker darkness settled again, her brother standing there, his hand on the shining neck of a restless mare, and beside him Susan Lathrop, her figure like an hourglass in the dark riding habit of the early nineties, her reddish gold hair curling under the stiff brim of her hat, her face vivid with laughter. She was more alive than anyone I ever knew, thought Margaret. Now she's a raddled old woman. They say she dyes her hair and paints her face. After all, I don't want to see her. It's been years —

But in July, when Margaret just missed seeing her, she was conscious for days of her disappointment. It gnawed at her when she woke up at night, when she lay waiting for seven o'clock to come, so that she had a reason for getting up. If only she hadn't been pampering herself, if she had gone in to the village shopping, if she had been working around the place, instead of staying in bed! She had caught cold, it had rained so many days in July that she had grown careless about keeping her feet dry, she had felt feverish, she had put herself to bed in a small panic. She couldn't afford to be sick, she had to keep herself well, she had to go back to school in the fall. She had, from her ground-floor rear bedroom, not heard any car drive along the grass-grown gravel road to the Lathrop house. When her own doorbell had rung, she had lain very still, waiting for whoever it was to go away. The next day the boy came to cut the grass; the steady rains made it grow almost faster than he could run the lawn mower. She listened to him for a while, following him about the familiar ground by the variations in the noise he made. When he reached the final square of grass behind the house, she got up, feeling exactly like an old dishrag; she meant to dress, but the labor seemed stupendous. She guessed it wouldn't hurt the boy to see her in a bathrobe, not after some of the sights he saw at Grady's beach. But she took off the net she had tied over her hair, and combed the waves carefully into place. Even her hair looked sick, limp, flattened to her small head. She made herself tea and toast, she wrote a list of supplies for the chain grocery store in the village, they wouldn't deliver unless she ordered two dollars worth, but perhaps Sam could bring the things out for her. Then, with her purse, she went to the kitchen door as Sam ran the lawn mower into the shed.

"I thought I better cut it today," he said, "looks like more rain." Sure, he'd bring out the groceries, he was going to the rink tonight anyways. Then he added, "Too bad you wasn't home yesterday. You sure missed a treat." He put the list in the pocket of his blue shirt, and slid the four quarters into a trouser pocket. "I was at the garage when she came back, see? They stopped for gas."

"Who did?" (I'm glad I didn't answer the doorbell, it must have been one of the girls from the school.)

"Old Mrs. Field, you know, the one used to live out here. She asked Bill did he know where you were, and he said he guessed you were home, you always was. She said you must be dead if you was here, not to hear her ring. She's kinda deaf, you have to holler at her, or mebbe it's her earrings, they're big as a traffic light. 'Who's living in the farmhouse?' she said, 'and where are they?' Bill said Miss Turner, and I guess she's home. She said, 'Turner? Turner? I've heard that name somewhere.' She was sitting up front with the chauffeur, he was a dark looking fellow, like a dago —"

"Is that all she said? What did she want?"

"The chauffeur said, we can't hang around here any longer, and he let the clutch in so hard the old dame bounced back with her hat over one eye. Honest, Miss Turner, you oughta see her! Dolled up like a mo'om picture star."

"What did she want of me?" Margaret's throat was dry.

"Gee, I don't know. Bill says just as well you wasn't home, you wouldn't want any truck with that piece of goods." The boy was grinning a little, his sandy, immature face touched with slyness, at the recollection of some male ribaldry he wouldn't repeat. Margaret could see it, in the way he glanced at her under his lids, in the way he rubbed a finger against a spot on his chin. She couldn't say go on, tell me every word he said, for she was parched with thirst for more than this sip of news. She nodded, her eagerness burning in her cheeks, her silence coaxed the boy. "It wasn't even the same fellow she had last time she stopped here. Bill said he was a light-complected fellow, and anyway his picture was in the papers, you know, when his wife chased 'em across the country and was going to shoot him, only Mrs. Field gave her about twenty grand and she divorced him instead. Bill says boy friends come kinda high at her age, and what's she going to do when her money gives out?"

(You shouldn't stand here gossiping with a village boy! It's horrid, undignified.) Margaret could hear the rebuke faintly, as if her usual decent self, the one she offered to public view, had withdrawn almost beyond inner earshot. And then, at the queer smirk the boy's face wore, she had a quick revulsion, a protest of her sex against the bawdiness at which she could only guess that must have shouted in Bill's actual remarks.

"She has to have a chauffeur," she said, crisply. "You don't know —"

"Huh, if you'd heard the way he spoke to her!" But Sam could take a hint, if Miss Turner didn't want any more it was okay with him. He stood away from the door against which he had lounged, he said, "I'll leave the groceries when I come by after supper, you send word by the postman if you want me before next week." Then he had gone.

Margaret sat down at the table in her quiet kitchen. She poured a cup of tea, but it had grown luke-warm, and she could not anywhere find energy to rise, to light the gas under the kettle. Painted, bedizened Jezebel, she thought. The village loafers making lewd sport of her. Well, Bill and Sam weren't exactly loafers, but the idea was the same. She thought she'd heard the name Turner! Why, she must have lost her mind. Perhaps that was the explanation. How could she have forgotten — Anger tightened in Margaret. Perhaps Susan Lathrop had never known we had a family name! An anger of her childhood, bitter, seeming when she first knew it entirely futile, and yet serving as a drive through the hard years as she had struggled upward. "It does you no good to kick against the station in life you're born to," her father used to say to her. "Even the prayer book tells you that!" Well, she was Miss Turner now to the village, and Susan Lathrop had turned into *that piece of goods*. For all Margaret's father had been Rob, never Mr. Turner, and her brother had been Bobby as he grew old enough to help his father with the gardens and horses, and she herself had been Maggie, loathing the name. The village men spoke of her with respect, she wouldn't want any truck with that piece of goods. And Susan, bright, beautiful, vivid Susan — Margaret pushed her hair away from her forehead, she sat very straight in the wooden chair. Susan Lathrop hadn't lost her mind, she'd lost her character.

Had she thought, because she moved so much about the earth, never staying long in any place, never in any way settling down, that rumors of her affairs would never reach as far as her home town? Or hadn't she cared, the headstrong, willful pride of the young Susan changed into the base alloy of arrogance and indifference? But there was no safety in distance any more, there was no distance any more. Any criminal must have a harder time now, thought Margaret. Why, when I was a girl, Boston seemed a long journey from here, or New York, people went there and the miles between were a cloak behind which they could hide. No one knew you. Rumor went on foot then, now it leaps at the turn of a dial, it shouts from the front page of a tabloid almost before the deed shouted has taken place. Margaret had saved the papers — more than a year ago, it was — although she meant to burn them. Deserted wife pursues mate across country, charges alienation of affection, says Mrs. Susan Lathrop Field made gifts of jewelry and money to handsome young Bullett, tempted him. Pictures of Susan, of Bullett, of deserted wife, of tiny tots weeping for father to come home. "She lured him by luxury," says wife, "until he was no longer content with our humble home." Pictures of Mrs. Field's villa at Cannes, of her twenty-two-room cottage at Bar Harbor. And later, picture of injured wife, handkerchief to her eyes, check in her hand. Fifty-thousand-dollar balm, said the headline. "Money does not replace him, but I must think of my kiddies," says wife. Twenty thousand, they said in the village. Whatever it was, before the end of the summer the village had the end of that story. George Carter, who ran the village barber shop, and his wife Ella, who had the beauty parlor in the room back of the barber shop, took a two weeks' vacation touring the East; George wanted to borrow his brother's trailer, but Ella said no, she wanted a real vacation, and they had stopped at over-night camps all the way to Canada and back. Since George's father and his grandfather before him had worked in the Lathrop factory, where Susan's money came from, it was only natural for the Carters to make

127

Bar Harbor one of their stops. They drove past the twenty-two-room cottage, and Ella asked which was the most exclusive beauty shop, and went there for a manicure. She felt she owed it to her customers to pick up what hints about the trade she could. She didn't have her hair done, as they wouldn't give her a trade discount, even when she showed them one of her printed cards. But a manicure gives a better chance for looking around and talking. As soon as the operator found out she was from Eastbourne, she opened right up. (Ella herself had opened up as she set the wave in Margaret's hair.) Susan Field was one of their steady customers. Facials, mud packs, henna rinses, everything! And next to her Maker, if Miss Turner would pardon Ella for speaking right out, who knew more about a woman than the operators in her beauty parlor? Ella always said maybe the Lord made them, but she knew who made them over. And from what the Bar Harbor girl said, there wasn't much left of the original job on Susan Lathrop Field.

As soon as I'm over this cold, thought Margaret, suddenly, I must make an appointment with Ella Carter. I ought to get my hair back in shape before school begins, I put too much bluing in when I wash it myself. She didn't finish her thought, that Ella might have heard something, or George, something more than the boy Sam had reported. Instead, her mouth a thin, scornful line, she turned over in her mind fragments of the story Ella had repeated. Susan, waiting an hour or more in the beauty parlor, peering up and down the busy resort street, nowhere among the tourists' dusty cars, the vanished station wagons with Maine license plates, the gay sport cars, nowhere Susan's imported town car, nowhere the handsome Bullett. He'd come when he got ready, he'd been dating up the cashier at the drug store, or a waitress

128

at the café. He never kept them waiting in the evening! When he did come, finally, Susan never bawled him out a bit: she'd just say, oh, I got finished early, or did I make a mistake again, I meant to say twelve o'clock, and he'd grin out of one corner of his mouth. A terrible picture, of a woman terrified, jealous, helpless. You couldn't help liking her, the girl had said, for all she acted like an old fool. They hadn't heard about Bullett's wife until Ella told them, they thought that explained a good deal. Then toward the end of the summer, just a year ago, Bullett went off with a woman, someone who had a sportswear shop in Bar Harbor in the summer, in Palm Beach winters. He went in a new coupe Susan had bought him, and she set the police after him. But then Susan collapsed, two nurses, doctors, and she must have called off the police, for no one heard another word.

"George's father always said old Mr. Lathrop was a prince," Ella had finished. "It seems kinda too bad, doesn't it, when you think of the advantages she had and all? George says her father would turn over in his grave. What I tell George is I can't understand any woman not getting her fill of men before she gets to that age! Why, the Bar Harbor operator told me —" then Ella had stopped, with a clicking of her tongue, and Margaret understood that her own condition of refined spinsterhood made it impossible for Ella to tell her all she had heard, even when the part withheld might well be the most — well, say, revealing. Margaret had failed to find a phrase which would, with dignity and decorum, release Ella's tongue. So she had merely said, "Too bad? It's horrible. You read about such things, but you don't believe them. But to hear them about a woman you knew — No, I refuse to try to understand it."

129

Margaret's head ached, with her rehearsal of Ella's story, with the way her thoughts, like a flock of starlings, rushed at the news Sam had brought, scattered in a rush at some impulse of her will. Why should she care so much what Susan Field did? What if she had another — what had Sam called them — another boy-friend? Grotesque and fascinating. And none of your business, she told herself, getting to her feet. Only what had Susan wanted of her, why had she rung her bell?

The rain had started again, making a small pricking noise against the windowpanes. Margaret thought, I'll catch more cold sitting here in the damp, I must go back to bed. She moved softly, not to jar her head, and shivered as she stretched herself flat and drew a blanket up to her chin. If ever the sun came out again, she ought to air everything in the house. For a few moments she kept her mind busy hanging out blankets, emptying closets, even the cedar closet in the attic where she stored her winter clothes. You had to watch out for mildew. Then Susan came back, quite as if she brushed down all the dangling garments and confronted Margaret. Only Margaret couldn't see her clearly. The pictures in the tabloids had been chiefly hat and summer fur, a great collar of white fox. Not a trace of the Susan Margaret had known. When she tried to construct an image out of what she had heard, she got the face of Edna May Oliver. That was Sam's remark, dolled up like a mo'om pitcher star. Margaret had a picture of her, a stiff cardboard photograph, huge puffed sleeves, lace collar wired up under the ears, round eyes staring with innocence under a frontispiece of frizzed bangs. It was in the tray of the Saratoga trunk, in the small package of letters, receipts, account book, which had been sent home from Colorado when Robert died. I'd like to show it to her, thought Margaret fiercely. I'd like to say, Look what you've done to yourself! Perhaps it was as well no one had answered when Susan rang. Too much might have been said.

The gray and rain-drenched twilight deepened until the pattern of the flowered wall paper was lost, until the silver-backed brushes (a gift from a senior class two years ago) ranged on the pine chest had no reflection in the mirror above them, and the landscape painted at the top of the mirror blurred into the rest of the grayness. It was the same room where Margaret had slept as a child, with Robert in the room next, and her father and mother in the front room, which she had made over into her study. The darkness dissolved the pleasant changes she had made, she might have been lying in the narrow iron bed, the painted white commode in the corner, matting tacked over the floor. As a child, excited because Susan Lathrop was coming home from the Select School for Young Ladies, and Margaret, in a clean apron, her face scrubbed, her hair slicked back in two pigtails, could play croquet with her, could follow her about, somewhat dazzled at her bright daring. I'm not sure it's good for Maggie, she could remember her mother saying. She gets all stirred up, she may get notions — And her father, Maggie's got sense enough to know she can't have the things nor do the things Lathrop's daughter can. Even then Susan wanted Robert to play with them — and then Robert wouldn't play with girls. Later, excited again because Susan was coming home, but a different Susan when she came, her skirts long, her lovely hair tucked up at the back of her head, a Susan who didn't want to play with girls now, who wanted Robert to ride with her, who wanted Lester Field! And Margaret had lain sleepless, her young body pressed against the thin mattress so hard the springs of the old iron bed made little ping-sounds all night, her

131

mouth muffled against the pillow. And now Susan had come home again, if only for a moment, and Margaret lay sleepless. What was it like, at Susan's age, not to be done with — ah, you couldn't call it love!

I must be feverish. Margaret sat up indignantly, snapped on the light on the night table, shook two tablets from the aspirin bottle, swallowed them with a sip of water, looked about her room, at the prints on the walls, at the ruffled organdy curtains, at every sign of dignified accomplishment which would fix her in the present. She let the light burning, turning her face away from it, and presently slept. When she woke, the lamp was pale in morning light, and she knew she had been dreaming. Bits of the dreams stayed a moment, drifting on the waves of waking before they were submerged and lost, Susan running ahead of her over the rocky shore, laughing at something, Margaret hurrying after her, slipping, falling, and Robert's voice, or was it her father's? Then they were gone. Margaret snapped off the light. She couldn't remember any more of the dream. She could see the sky through the curtains, mother-of-pearl and lustrous, the rain had ended, she felt better. It was queer, how in dreams you never were any age, young, or middle-aged, or old, you were just you, all of you at once, some secret essence of you. Perhaps that was the way you ought to be, awake, only some foolish notion about time and years lived got in between you and yourself; or your waking memory was weak, holding today as the only real thing, while all of you was really there, continuous, and in dreams the whole you pressed through the barriers. But her thought was almost part of the dream, and as she woke fully, sank with the dream under the surface of her waking.

The next few days the sun shone coppery in a glazed sky, the breeze was feather-light and southerly, there seemed no air to breathe, just the warm mist which rose from the drenched earth. Margaret tried sunning her blankets, and found them at the end of the day so damp she could not fold them away. Her shoes, ranged neatly in shoe-rails on her closet door, had a patina of mildew on heels and soles. There was through the house the faint musty smell of fibers playing host to invisible and multiplying fungi, wood, plaster, rugs, everything. Even the books had a taint of this odor, and their covers bulged as if someone had left them in the grass all night. If it's like this in the tropics, thought Margaret, I'm glad I never went there. She felt a little as if her bones were mildewed, she couldn't throw off a heaviness of body or of spirit which her cold had left, she fretted against the weather as if it were a private enemy using unfair weapons like poison gas against her and her possessions. If it's this bad in my house, with everything open to what air there is, she thought, what must it be in the big house, all sealed shut. Someone ought to go in, to see what's happening. There had been elegant things in that house, Margaret remembered the red velvet portieres of the drawing room, the gold chairs with red velvet cushions, the crystal chandelier. She might write to Susan. Dear Susan, Perhaps you don't realize this is the worst summer we've ever had at the shore, no one ever saw anything like it, I don't know of course what you've left in your house, but it will certainly be ruined — Write her and be laughed at for her trouble. Susan was old enough to look out for her own things. But she never had looked out for things. Careless, generous. Well, she never had to work for anything, why shouldn't she be careless and generous?

Leaving her toys anywhere, tearing her dresses, giving away anything — Margaret had forgotten —

That little gold necklace, like a fine rope, with the locket, its blue enameled flower and a pearl for its center; Margaret had loved it. Susan had let her wear it one day, had said, keep it, you can have it. Margaret's mother had sent her scampering back with it, crying, her hand clutched over the locket as she climbed the steps to the kitchen door. "They'd think you stole it, a valuable piece of jewelry like that! I don't care if Susan did give it to you, she shouldn't have! Hurry up!" The cook had been cross. Miss Susan was having her bath, the cook had was busy with dinner, hadn't Maggie been playing with Miss Susan all day, this was no time to be bothering people. Margaret had marched home, she could keep the necklace over night, she could wear it under her nightgown, she couldn't see Susan before morning. But her mother had taken it off, it had caught in her hair and tweaked it cruelly; she had wrapped it in a bit of paper and sent Father straight off with it. "If they should think you took it! They'd never let you play with her again, they might not want us to stay here! You ought to know better, in our position." She had fairly flown at Father when he came back. "Well?" And Father, "I saw Lathrop, he just laughed and said that girl of his would give her head away if it wasn't riveted on." Susan had said she didn't see why Maggie's mother made such a fuss, but she'd give it back at Christmas. Only she had forgotten, by Christmas she was gone, just where that year Margaret didn't recall. You'll learn, Margaret's mother had said, that it isn't enough to know you are honest and right yourself, you have to see to it that what you do looks that way to everyone else. You can't be too careful. Advice, Margaret knew now, wrung from a stem that pricked with poverty

134

and hard work and insecurity. Not that there could have been any real threat that Rob Turner would lose his job; always Lathrop's projects, and he had new ones steadily, included Rob, no matter how far they reached into the future. But Mary Turner, Margaret's mother, had gone out to service when she was not yet thirteen, because her own mother had died, and her father, drawn as a vague, good-natured, shiftless figure in the few comments Margaret had ever heard, had taken one way of incompetents, and run away from the problem of his family. Mary Turner had learned early that providence was not to be trusted, and the rest of her life she forestalled any tricks it might play by anticipating the worst. A hard worker, and a harder worrier, Rob Turner used to say. Well, Margaret had remembered her advice; she had been careful, and Susan hadn't.

It was queer the way things kept coming back. Perhaps because she hadn't energy enough to stir around filling her hours with small tasks which took the place of thought. She read the Boston paper every day, walking slowly to the postbox for it after the mail truck passed. But China and Spain were shadows into which her imagination did not venture, and labor troubles were men who didn't have sense enough to stick to jobs when they had them, she might almost have been reading news about another planet, not the one on which she lived. In a way, she was, for all the portents of change had to do with a future world which could not trouble her for long. What she read had less substance than what she remembered. Perhaps the fact that Susan had rung her doorbell and gone away, her errand unexplained, perhaps that ringing of the bell had set in vibration, had waked echoes of Susan. If only I could get in town, thought Margaret, and see Ella; she might have heard more than Sam had

135

reported. But while this spell of weather lasted, she couldn't risk it, waiting at the roadside for a crowded bus, sitting in Ella's back room with the saturated air weighted still more with scented lotions. She could see her name in the list of heat prostrations.

At the end of the week, at the end of a day which seemed worse than the preceding days, intolerable because it was another of the same kind, the wind changed. Margaret was sitting in a canvas chair on the terrace at the side of her house, head back against the gay green and yellow stripes, eyes closed, hands listless. She had been thinking, I ought to go in and get some supper, I can't lie here forever. She heard the wind before she felt it, heard it in the treetops between her and the distant shore. She listened, it was almost like rain, the little swishing noise of leaves turning quickly against each other. She opened her eyes, the treetops, maples and oaks, were in motion, clouds had gathered behind them, the setting sun glinted through clouds, catching the pale under side of leaves as the wind ruffled them. Then she could smell it, an east wind strong with the odor of the salty water, the flats over which it blew. A change of wind, coming in with the tide. She sniffed it eagerly, she stood up to let it blow her thin silk skirt about her. It meant rain, but cooler weather, too. She might walk to the shore, it would be good to see something besides the flat, glassy sea of the past week. Ordinarily she disliked being blown upon, but this evening she stretched into the wind, she walked more springily into it, her usual crisp, rather prim step lengthening. There was no surf as yet, even on the rocky outer shore of the point; the surface of the bay was in motion, long ripples across its gray, and the tide spoke in hurried splashes about the rocks, its usual rhythm of withdrawal and approach lost in the wind's drive.

Margaret watched, and as the first large drops of rain fell starting and cold on her head and face, she turned back. She had to run for her house, past the dark sealed Lathrop house, under the uneasy trees, and as she ran, Susan was running beside her, her flying bright hair darkening as the rain drenched them both. Margaret reached her door, stopped, leaning against it until her heart stopped its thumping; when had she and Susan run through the rain? Susan, with something in her arms, drabbled, dirty-white, blood-smeared, held firmly against Susan's white dress, a nondescript little dog, its side torn, one leg dangling limp. It tried feebly to lick its side, Susan panted, "I can't run any more, I jiggle it too much." Margaret had seen it first, cowering under a rock in the corner of the field, just the briefest glance had shown her its terrified and pain-glazed eyes, she had looked away, hastily, wanting not to see it, not to have to know what it was, and called out to Susan, "I'll race you to the road." But Susan had seen it, had flung herself down beside it, dropping the rope of daisies and sweet clover the two of them had braided, had made soft, compassionate noises in her throat, stretching her hands out slowly, and the dog's lip had curled back from its teeth. "Leave it alone, Susan! He'll bite you! He's dreadful, you mustn't touch him!" Susan had not even heard her, after a moment she had one hand on his head, smoothing the dirty skin over the patient, rounded skull, and then she was hoisting herself to her feet, the animal clasped against her body. "He's been hurt," she said, in a whisper, as if she didn't want the dog to hear. "Oh, let's hurry! Your father will know what to do, Maggie." Then the rain, the threat of which had started them homeward, had begun to fall, and they had run, Margaret gulping the bitter lump of shame she would not admit, telling herself, I didn't know it was hurt,

137

not really, anyway it isn't safe, he might bite, look at her pretty dress — Susan had never said once, didn't you see him lying there? Margaret's father had dressed the wound, had put a splint on the leg. "He must of had a fight, dogs, or maybe a bobcat." Presently he was hobbling after Susan, his long cur tail flailing the air. He wouldn't come near Margaret, he rolled his yellowish hound-dog eyes, showing the whites, when he saw her. It was too much as if he said, if Susan knew what I know, she wouldn't think much of you! After Susan had left that fall, the dog had disappeared. "He had the makings of a good hunting dog," said Margaret's father, "but he had a roving foot."

Margaret hadn't thought of that dog for years, it couldn't be guilt now which felt so dry in her throat, she'd just lost her breath, running. She didn't worry now what Susan Lathrop Field thought of her! She must take off her dress, lucky she'd had on this old wash-silk. She could light a small fire in the fireplace, it would be pleasant with the rain outside.

When, at the end of the next week, Margaret rode in to the village on the bus, she found George Carter's assistant in charge of the barber shop, and the door to Ella's beauty parlor closed, with a sign, "Back in two weeks." "They just jumped in the car the minute they saw the sun," explained the strange young man.

"I should think Ella might have let her customers know." Margaret was resentful. "Here I came way in on purpose —"

"She talked some of putting in a girl while she was gone, but she said she just lost money when she did, you ladies wouldn't have anyone but her. Now with men it's different, a shave's a shave and you gotta have it when you gotta have it." He bulged comfortably under his white cotton jacket, but his enjoyment of his own comment did not soften Margaret's little scowl of disappointment. "They've gone to see her folks," he added. "Her mother's poorly, that's one reason she was in a hustle to get away."

Then Ella would have no news when she came back. Margaret edged away from the door; she oughtn't to be standing looking into a men's barber shop. The young fellow didn't look after her as she went along the street, stepping precisely in her carefully whitened canvas oxfords, the bright sun bringing out a faint odor of cleaning fluid from the white front of her figured blue silk dress. Two hours until a bus left for Grady's Amusement Park, the bus which ran past her door. She prolonged her few errands, crossing off each item from her list as she bought it, a spool of darning cotton, toilet soap (she was firm with herself about that, she liked good soap, scented, Yardley's or Houbigant's, she mustn't be extravagant, after all she'd practically wasted her bus fare today). The drugstore clerk said, "Nice to see the sun again," and she agreed. In the grocery store she removed her white cotton gloves to pinch the lettuce heads, the clerk said, "Nice to see the sun again," and she agreed, selecting the firmest head.

There were so many strangers in town in the summer, she really didn't know anyone in the village now. When she'd gone away to college, those long years of hard work, teaching in a country school, a year at a normal, another year of teaching, steady up-climb, she'd lost touch with people here. All her friends now were in the city, she told herself, why should this feeling, like a vague homesickness, pull at her eyelids, at the corners of her mouth? Just because she had to wait for the bus, feeling sorry for herself that there was nowhere in the village a door where she might present herself, where someone

139

would say, "Why, Margaret Turner, come in! How are you? How nice to see you!" Some of the girls she had known in school had married and settled here, she wouldn't know them if she met them, grandmothers now, or dead, some of them. There weren't any of them I cared about, she thought; they were all dull — after Susan. And my life was different, I made it different. She straightened her shoulders, she thanked the clerk for the neat heavy paper bag with string handles into which she could drop all her small purchases. When he said, "I suppose you won't be here much longer, Miss Turner? You'll be getting back to the city?" she almost thanked him again, he had in a phrase restored her.

"I'll be here the rest of August, at least," she said. "I'm not sure just when I have to leave. September's such a lovely month at the shore."

He waited politely for her to finish, ignoring for the moment the Italian woman, her uncovered dark hair in a loose knot in the plump ridge of her neck, who was shaking a banana at him and saying how mucha, how mucha; he was a nice young man, thought Margaret, as she stepped crisply out of the store.

She walked to the garage, to leave word for Sam. Tomorrow was his regular day, he might have come anyway, but leaving word was one more errand. Bill, in boots and rubber apron, had a car on the washing stand. He held the hose away from Margaret, touched his green eye shade with wet fingers. "You don't want a taxi yet, Miss Turner?"

"Not just yet." Bill made it sound like a friendly joke; he drove her to the station with her trunk and bags, when she left in the fall, he drove her home again in the spring, but he always mentioned the taxi, quite as if she might recklessly order one out at any time. She explained about

140

Sam, and Bill thought he'd probably see the kid, he hung around a lot.

She could see the mouth of the river through the rear door of the garage, with a coal barge drawn up along the dock. "Nice to see the sun again," said Bill, as she walked away. She thought of Susan's shining car standing near the red gasoline pump, and Bill beside it, his shrewd, homely, grimy face puckered with that expression she had seen in Sam's eyes. If Susan didn't know how they — yes, leer was the word for it! — how they all leered at her very name, it was high time someone told her.

Still an hour to wait before the bus came. Margaret went slowly along the narrow street which edged the river, the old docks and piers on one side, a row of one-story wooden buildings on the other, half of them closed, tattered advertisements of beer or tobacco tacked on the boards nailed over the old windows. When she was a child, this was the busiest street in town, with saloons, The Sailors' Snug Harbor, The Oasis, with lunch places, shops smelling of tarred rope and metal; no nice girl ever walked down it alone, even to look at the lumber schooners, the fishing sloops, which lay along the wharves, the girls who did walk there didn't go to look at the ships. Behind one dusty window was a pile of slickers, straddled by a pair of black fisherman's boots, farther along a sign above a door said BEER, but for the most part the street was abandoned, as were the docks. Almost, thought Margaret, as if the sea had retired from business. Motor vans boomed along highways with the freight now, the sons and grandsons of the sailors and fishermen worked in the factories back from the waterfront, or didn't work on W.P.A. projects. She walked, placing her white shoes with caution on worn planks, out to the end of the longest pier, the one from which the excursion

141

steamer used to run. When they'd opened Grady's Amusement Park, they had painted the little steamer shining white, and advertised moonlight sails to the Park. But who wanted a slow boat, a crowd of people? Margaret had heard stories of what went on in the cars parked along the beaches. She looked at the ticket office, the locked turnstile, the blank window, and then seated herself on the wooden bench.

Her father had taken them on a Sunday excursion once; she must have been very young, for she could remember her brother Robby in a round straw hat and a sailor collar. She had been seasick, she could smell now the dust-stuffy, pricky smell of the green plush on the seat in the ladies' cabin where she had lain miserably, her mother sitting beside her. Why, that was the real reason — She stared at the water, dark, an oily iridescence in the eddies it made around the end piles of the pier — That time Lester Field had asked her to go — if she had gone, her whole life would have been different. She couldn't exactly see his face, not as he had been then; superimposed upon the young face was the face of the older Lester as she had seen him just once, twenty years later, a face of heavy whitish flesh, like wax, with irresolute mouth and dull eyes, the underlids sagging. He had been killed hunting, that fall. Drunk, they said. Well, he married Susan for her money and she gave him a run for it. The village talked thus about Susan even then, almost thirty years ago.

All Margaret could catch now of the young face was the heavy stroke the eyebrows made, the imperious stare of the dark eyes, the assurance of his smile. He had finished law school, he had come back to town to spend the summer in his father's office, he had come out to the farm with some papers for her father to sign, he had seen

Margaret, he had come back, often. "He's hanging around too much," her mother had said. "I don't like it. I wouldn't like him anyway, and you have to face the fact he's not the same class, and that just means trouble." Margaret couldn't listen to her. (What a sweet baby you are, Margie! Kiss me! What's the harm?) Where, in her staid, neat body lingered the echo of that ecstasy? Lester had planned the whole thing. A friend of his, and his girl. Margaret could tell her mother she was spending the night with her — and now she couldn't remember the girl's name! There was a full moon. Lots of good places on the old boat where no one can see us, just you and me, Margie, and the moon and the water! Margaret had refused. I couldn't, Lester. It wouldn't be right. She had been faint with longing to go, she had consoled herself in bitter days afterwards that at least she had resisted temptation, she had lived up to her standards. A gull circled over her, so near she saw its round bright eye, and its cry as it swooped away was like a derisive laugh. *Aorr,* he screamed, that's how you kept your virtue, afraid you would be seasick! Had that been the reason, or was this only an ironic trick of her nerves, this lonely afternoon? Lester had been angry; before Margaret saw him again, Susan had come home from abroad. If I had gone with him that night, he was angry because he thought I did not care enough for him — He had begun to love me — I could have held him, in spite of Susan.

Margaret got to her feet, her paper bag crackled against her knee, she set her mouth firmly, what possessed her, harking back to all these old, long-lived-past moments? She was like those gulls, walking with their stiff ungraceful balance at the edge of the receding tide, under the shored-up bank from which the pier ran out, pecking over the marginal debris. The odor of the water was strong in her nostrils, brackish, fishy, town-tainted, unlike the clean salt pungency of her own shore. She wouldn't come in town again unless she had to; she didn't like it.

Nor did she care much for the bus ride to her door. She stared out of the rattling, half-opened window, trying not to be in any way a part of the company in which she rode, women in flowered beach pajamas, in slacks, their rotundities bulging comfortably, bandannas, not too clean, tied under their chins, the ends wagging with gum-chewing and shrill talk, grubby children scrabbling all over the seats, half naked, scratches on their sunburned legs. Too early for the night crowd at Grady's, these were part of the colony this side of Grady's Park, summer cottages to rent by week or month, they rode in to the village movies as often as the bill changed. Riff-raff. Margaret hadn't been along the shore as far as the cottages since they were first built; she'd heard they were run down, rents had been reduced, the owner couldn't half fill the places, families didn't take vacations any more. A shame they'd let people like that in, lowering the tone of the place. That was the first property Susan's agent had sold, Susan had pocketed the money without the least concern what happened to the land. There was distance enough between Margaret's house and the cottages so that she seldom saw the inhabitants, except on such a bus ride. But she thought how nice it would have been to have two or three pleasant summer homes along the shore, with what she called desirable people; she could have called on them, they could have dropped in to see her. One of the children stopped beside her seat, a scrawny little girl, the scanty front of her playsuit sagging away from her flounder-flat front. She was working on an ice-cream cone, boring a hole with her tongue in the melting chocolaty mound, she stared with shrewd, pale eyes under wisps of sun-bleached hair at Margaret. The bus bounced off the edge of the pavement, passing a car, and back again, the child fell in against Margaret's knee, Margaret's quick hand pushed child and dripping cone away, they were a heap at her feet, sticky cone planted on her ankle, a startled *awk* from the child. Margaret contracted, a violent physical withdrawal, at this violation of her privacy, her isolation, her very cleanliness. "Look what you've done, you bad little girl!" she said, fiercely. The child was hoisting her pointed stern, a gurgle of despair coming from near the dirty bus floor. She couldn't make it, what with the narrow space, the jerking of the bus. Margaret leaned forward, she had to do something, she slid her hands along the thin, smooth back, she pulled the child up. Amazingly, the child settled on the seat beside her, leaning against Margaret's arm, wedging what was left of the ice cream into the cone again with dirty fingers, proceeding solemnly to lap it with her pointed tongue. I had forgotten how small a child's arm feels, how small and hard a child's body, light, warm, like a little unfeathered bird —

"Ardelia, you come here, stop bothering the lady, you come here, I say!"

Ardelia slid to the floor, her eyes holding to Margaret's face for a moment, with that shrewd, unblinking stare, almost as if she measured the confusion Margaret felt. What nonsense, thought Margaret, dabbing with a Kleenex at the smudge on her ankle, then jerking at the bell cord. The bus driver watched her in his mirror, he pulled to a stop, and she climbed stiffly down, not looking once at anyone in the bus as she left. She was a dirty little thing, thought Margaret, angrily. Her arm still kept that pressure, warm, light, those small, smooth

145

bones. Lucky that mess didn't land on my dress, I'll have to change my stockings. What was the matter today, that loneliness should take so many forms to trip her? Her house waited for her, charming, quiet, its own shadow from the low sun stretching dark across the lawn almost to her feet. The tin flag on her postbox was down, she opened the front and took out not only the daily paper, but two letters. One had the school address smartly printed on the flap. She didn't recognize the writing on the other. As she fitted her key into the lock, she told herself firmly, your holiday is almost over, you should be enjoying it instead of having such megrims. She had heard somewhere that these summer colds left you depressed, a kind of poison in the system. Maybe she should get a tonic.She put away her purchases methodically, she set her hat on the padded hat-tree in the hall closet, and then she went into the living room with paper and letters. Her reading glasses were in a drawer of the desk; she seated herself in the armchair near a window, and waited a moment, hoping for the surge of comfort which homecoming should bring, a moment to feel that warm recognition that she, Margaret Turner, had done this for herself, gained for herself this setting, this position. But today she was uneasy. She turned the letter from the school in her fingers, she found it lightly sealed, and ran her thumb under the flap. Just a note, she thought, about which day she should appear for conferences with parents.

She read the letter twice, with no shock, rather with feeling that she had read it before, that she had known all day, all summer, that it would lie in her postbox, awaiting her. The Head Mistress of the school knew that Margaret would understand, she was sorry to write so late, but probably Margaret would be relieved that she could now stay in her charming home, in the spring she had thought the budget for salaries was properly balanced, but one or two bad investments, if any investments nowadays were anything but bad, and so forth. The point being, at the end of the third page, that Lucy Alder, the assistant, could handle all the classes in mathematics, and Margaret needn't come back. Be sure to keep in touch with us, with deep appreciation of your splendid service.

Margaret folded the letter along the creases, but she couldn't get it to slide into the envelope, it crackled and would not go in. She laid it beside her on the table, moving her hand cautiously, as if something slept here in the house which a sudden movement, a noise, might waken. Still quietly she opened the second letter, and looked at the printed circular which the non-revealing envelope contained, her face creasing wryly. Strictly confidential, to teachers, loans arranged, no other security required, no signatures except your own, absolute privacy. Teachers were all hard up, then. Or they were easy marks. But she wasn't a teacher any more, didn't they understand? Then she unfolded the newspaper, spread it on her knees. The words were there under her eyes, but they were only marks, signifying nothing. So she sat still, her hands lying on the paper, open, empty, inert. The light in the room changed, as the sun dropped under the horizon. A soft afterglow made amber highlights on polished surfaces of wood, tinted the pale ground of the chintz curtains, lay for a moment across Margaret's hands.

I might as well get my supper, she said, presently. I can't do anything about it, not tonight, anyway. If she moved softly, she wouldn't rouse the thing that slept, she knew its shape, but she could pretend she didn't know it was there at all. It stirred as she went into the kitchen,

147

with her thought: I can make the payment on the mortgage this fall, the tax bill at the end of September, but then what do I eat, what do I burn for warmth? Oh, not tonight! I have time enough to plan, to figure out a way — Time? She stumbled, and her hand clung against the paneling of the door.

* * * * *

By the middle of September Margaret had reached a cessation of worry. At least, the part of her mind that tried to look ahead, to plan, had stopped its endless fumbling search for a way out, after it had worn smooth the walls of the dark and narrow shaft into which she had been plunged, and found no crack. She had tried several things. She had made a package of the few bits of jewelry she owned, an old watch of her father's in a hunting case, earrings of her mother's, a diamond stick-pin that had come with the letters and photograph from Robert's landlady; she had taken the train one wet day early in September to the city, and after walking past the doorway three times, had forced herself into the pawnbroker's shop, past the counters of revolvers, musical instruments, clocks and candlesticks, to the dusty, railed office at the rear. The proprietor, like a queer beetle with his magnifying lens for an eye, offered her four dollars for the lot, and that's more than they're worth. Without a word she had wrapped them again in tissue paper and walked out. She had then written to Martha Miller, the plump ex-teacher who had wanted to visit her in the summer, suggesting that if Martha hadn't found a place to spend the winter, she might like to stay with Margaret. If I furnish the house, and you pay for the food — She sent the letter in care of the school, and two days later it came

148

back, with a note from the secretary. Dear Miss Turner, No one seems to have Miss Miller's address, if I hear I'll let you know.

She had thought she might get some teaching to do in the village schools. Not full time, she'd retired because she didn't wish to go back to the city, but a class in algebra, perhaps, or tutoring, a few hours a week. She was sorry she had made the inquiry, she dwindled and aged so under the apathetic stare of the superintendent, a youngish man with large hands from which the coat sleeves rode up. "Just a sort of busman's holiday," she had said, brightly. "After so many years —" They had a waiting list, girls from Normal School; he didn't know whether they could even keep the schools open all winter, he'd heard rumors —

She had finally, with a fluttering desperation which made her talk too fast and give breathless little laughs, gone to the real estate office in the village. She had retired, she explained, to the portly man with ashes on his vest, who had laid down his cigar, taken off his hat, and tipped his chair forward at her entrance. She thought she might like to spend the winter in town, at a good boarding house, did he think he could rent her house, he knew it, very desirable, of course she wouldn't want a family, a large family — He had picked up his unlighted cigar, poked it into a corner of his mouth, and tipped his chair back. How much did she expect? Nobody would want to go out there for the winter, he didn't know as they would even in the summer, he'd put it on the list, property out that way wasn't worth much, folks just wanted a bed and a bath-house. He chewed reflectively, rubbing a finger over the crease in his bald forehead. "I tell you, Mrs. Turner," he said, "the trouble is, they ain't no money now, folks haven't found what to use *for* money."

149

When Margaret opened the door of her house that evening, she felt apologetic; she had offered it to vandals, and even that had been of no use. When she wrote the check for the mortgage payment, she folded the checkbook hastily and shut it away in a drawer, before her eye, so used to figures, could give her the balance left.

The Labor Day weekend ended the season for Grady's Park. The fireworks woke Margaret from a light, uneasy sleep, she heard cars passing all night. After that, the families moved away from the shore, driving past in laden sedans, mattresses rolled and tied on top, baby carriages and chairs wobbling at the side. School had opened, summer was over, everyone had a place to go, had to go, except Margaret. She was restless, the thin, high, valiant call of migrant birds flying under the night sky, which she heard in her wakeful hours, was like the voice of her own need to be off, to be fitted again into the routine of work. She told herself she was glad she didn't have to walk through those chattering crowds of girls, to try to keep order in study period, to explain the square of a plus b, or what x equals to young things for whom x equalled only swing music and a movie hero and love. If she could remember how wretched she had always been just at this time in September, when she had set the house in order and closed it for the winter! For a day or so she waited eagerly for the postman. Perhaps the Head Mistress would write saying that after all she needed Margaret, Lucy Alder had been taken sick, or married, or registration was so heavy. But never did Margaret think of writing to the school, Look, I've worked all these years for you, I don't know where to turn — She couldn't destroy the pleasant picture of Margaret Turner, gentlewoman, with background, home, enviable, independent. She was detached now, floating in unreality, but if she destroyed that picture she had allowed them to construct of her, what would she be? She knew exactly how they would shove her into oblivion. No one could afford sympathy in these days; if you seemed an object for — not even sympathy, just reasonable assistance — the technique was to turn upon you, accusingly. You should have known better, you should have made provision; they tied the guilt about your neck like a flat-iron, and pushed you out of sight. That way you no longer troubled them. Look at Martha Miller, they didn't even know where she was! And Simmsy, and the others. At least, thought Margaret, I can keep my pride.

She found it hard to keep the picture of herself clear. She missed the casual inquiries, did you have a pleasant summer, you must have, of course, in that sweet house of yours, I suppose you just hated to come away, back to the same old grind. She said, I'm just restless because I've had to get to work so many years, when I get used to it — Sometimes her head felt curiously light, as if indeed she floated, the pull of gravity gone, as if she were in fact detached from the earth. Perhaps she wasn't eating enough, although she thought, I must keep up my strength, I mustn't get sick. She told Sam he needn't come again, grass didn't have to be cut in September, and then the persistent rains made the lawns as lush and green as in June. She pushed the lawn mower herself, leaning against the wooden handle, her heart whirring like the blades. The thick foliage of the wet summer still clung green to all the trees, almost as if the change of season had failed for them as well as for Margaret. No use worrying, she thought, woman or tree; there is nothing to be done about it. Nothing.

Her subscription to the newspaper expired on the eighteenth and she didn't renew it. Extraordinary, how

151

many things she had spent money for which she didn't need. With no paper, she could omit that trip to the postbox, trailing through the incessant rain, feeling the sodden ground suck at her feet, the gusty wind pluck at her umbrella. They should have a spell of bright, warm weather after the deluge. She didn't like to start making fires yet, if she was careful, she could get along for weeks and weeks on the wood stacked in the wood-shed. She could bring up driftwood for the fireplace, if ever it dried out.

She hadn't thought of Susan Lathrop Field since the letter from the school. For one thing, the rain had kept her from walking past the old house to the shore; for another, the letter had for a time wrenched her out of the past, even out of the present, had knocked her flat against the solid, crackless future. But when she woke Wednesday morning, she knew she had been dreaming again of Susan. A young Susan, saying, "You're so smart, Margaret, only you're scared of things." Had she ever said that, or had the dream only remembered some impatient moment when Susan tried to urge the child Maggie into action? I'm not scared any more, thought Margaret, surprised. She could move her mind into the place where fear had dwelt, and feel its emptiness, much as she might run her tongue into the gap where an aching tooth had been drawn. I wish I could see Susan, before — She stopped again, not defining that *before*. There was no rain against the windows, but the light within the room had an irregular pulsing change, from dull shadow to a quick pearl-gray, almost a hint of sun, and then to shadow again. Margaret stood at a window, tying her bathrobe cord. The vault of the sky had an uneasy counterpoint, high, thin dark clouds sweeping northward, like strokes from a fine brush, lower, cottony masses of clouds drifting

152

more lazily toward the south, and from the rocky shore the pounding of waves. Perhaps the rainy spell was breaking up, she thought, she might walk down to see the surf.

She bathed and dressed quickly; she couldn't dally in the morning, she'd had too many years of training. It seemed warm enough for a summer frock, recklessly she took from her neat closet a white linen dress, recklessly because she would have to launder it herself. But she liked to iron; there was a simple pleasure in subduing wrinkled cloth to perfect smoothness. The whiff of heated cotton, of starch, of bees-wax in the scorched pad, was in her nostrils, she remembered it as the smell of pride itself, the day she had been promoted from sheets and towels, her mother had allowed her to iron one of Father's shirts, white, with tucked bosom, she had stood on a box beside the ironing board, she could hear the *szz* with which the iron spat at her moistened finger-tip. Later moments of achievement had never surpassed that one.

The green belt was loose about her waist; that was good. She'd always put on weight in the fall, eating those elaborate luncheons in the school dining room. The final glimpse of herself in the mirror — even her hair looked better this morning, shining-white, the ends tucked under and pinned, she was getting so she did it pretty well herself — gave her an unexplained feeling of anticipation. There's nothing that can happen, she thought. Nothing left to happen to me. But she moved more lightly than she had for days, setting her bedroom in order, turning back sheets and blankets over a chair to air, preparing tea and toast for her breakfast. Whenever she listened, she could hear the waves down on the shore, but she postponed the walk she had promised herself, saying, first I will do this, and that. Be a good girl and finish your work first, then

153

you can go and play. She smiled, hearing the words from her childhood. She had neglected her house lately, running around on footless errands. Not that anything was dusty; the rains had prevented that. But this morning every polished surface had a dulling over it, as if the day had laid a warm mouth close and blown upon it. Margaret rubbed tables and chairs and floors bright again, she wiped off the inside of the small-paned windows. Once or twice the sun shone out, several times the rain started again, an onslaught of long, slanting lines which stopped abruptly. When Margaret had finished the stint she had set herself, well past noon, the rain seemed to have ceased, and as she stood at her front door, the raincoat over her arm beating in the wind, she saw how shadows of torn clouds moved swiftly over the sun-lit landscape, like waves of an advancing tide of night. She hesitated a moment, because the wind was strong, but the surf pounded loud, and she thought, I ought to see it, I don't remember ever hearing it so loud.

She had to step back inside the hall to get her arms into the sleeves of the raincoat, she tied a scarf over her head, she locked her door and hid the key under one of the stones that bordered the row of tattered perennial stalks, glancing first up and down the deserted highway to make sure no one watched. Then she pushed herself into the wind, she leaned against it, breathing hurt, it was a great hand laid against her chest, pressing it back against her spine. She reached the shelter of the old barn, and stopped, gasping. She could breathe there, and the air tingled to the tips of her fingers. She wouldn't be beaten by a few gusts, she meant to look at the water. The ground was littered with leaves, they ran on the wind, not single and brown as in the fall, but torn clumps, branches of green leaves. Behind her the wind scooped at the barn roof, and old gray shingles flew off, no noisier than the leaves. Presently she went on, turning sidewise, ducking her head. The house afforded another lee, as she passed it, she walked close to it, liking the space of silence under the walls, the noise and the wind came over the roof like a wave, not touching her, breaking farther out in the great trees. She ducked her head again, wading through the long wet grass toward the shore, and suddenly, although the sun shone now, her face was wet, her lashes were beaded. She tasted salt on her lips, and saw the spray break above the rocks. Queer, because the tide was low now, she had looked it up in her almanac that morning, she had thought the rain had stopped as the tide ebbed. Instead, even on the sheltered shore where the bath-house stood, the waves broke higher than the top step, the air was full of salt spray, stinging her eyelids so that she could scarcely see the craziness of the water beyond the point. That's very queer, she thought. I must have made a mistake, it's high tide now. She rubbed her eyelids dry. The reef which made the extension of the rocky shore beyond the point, and protected the harbor side, was now so submerged it had no line of breakers, and as Margaret stared, one wave — a seventh wave, she thought, remembering a bit of child lore — rushed up, a splendid smooth wall of green, over the rocks, broke into white over the grass, and crawled back as if discomfited at the strange contact. Then, without a sound above the wind and water, the old bath-house rose slowly, a foot or two, and lurched forward, flattening like a cardboard box, sliding out uncertainly as the beach was sucked bare between waves. A huge cloud shadow moved over the water, dimming the brilliant green and white to gray, almost to black, it covered the land, too, and Margaret turned inland. If it meant to rain again, she had better

155

hurry back to her house. It would be less lonely inside a house; the curious excitement of anticipation which had carried her since waking, like a wave, had broken all about her feet into complete solitude. She had just taxed herself too much, fighting the wind. It was behind her now, she went quickly with it, head down, she felt flat as paper, the wind carrying her along. When she reached the old house, she would stop for a moment on the kitchen porch, to rest.

She saw, not believing, that the long weathered green shutters of the drawing room at the corner of the house were open. Had the wind — Then she saw that the inner blinds were folded back, a figure moved within the room. The wind swept her on, in spite of her desire to stand there, staring, around the corner of the house. The side door, under the porte-cochere, was open, a man stood there, poised in haste to be off, a youngish stocky man with a brimmed cap pushed back on his head. Margaret had a good look at him, square forehead, handsome eyes under full lids, a young mouth twisted impatiently, a short, round chin that jutted well forward.

"What do you want to stay here for?" he was saying. "Come along with me now, and save me the trip back."

"It won't take you ten minutes to drive out for me." The voice came from within the hall, and at its sound, full, rich, amused, Margaret lifted her head, moved a step nearer, leaning stiffly against the push of the wind. "Run along, darling."

"You're crazy! A day like this —"

"It's a nice day, Eddie. Exciting, here at the shore. I won't go sit in that garage while you tinker over the car. I'll look for that box I told you about. Why, maybe I won't go with you when you come back!"

Eddie's face changed, it was impudent and cajoling. "You promised!"

"Before I came back here, came — home. I had forgotten —" The voice drew Margaret to the edge of the steps. Eddie shrugged, he flung up one hand as the elm behind him bent in the wind and straightened again, with a noise through all its wet leaves like the tearing of paper. "Listen to that! I don't like it!" he cried out, "I don't like leaving you!" Then he saw Margaret. As he stared, a figure moved through the doorway to stand on the narrow porch, a plump figure stepping briskly on small feet in high-heeled wine-colored sandals, a wine-colored coat fluttering as the wind caught it, the long bands of golden lynx flattening in the wind, the chiffon veil which tied on the brimmed hat moving, and there, above the fur, under the hat, a small face, pointed, wrinkled, with an astonishing russet rim of curled hair, with eyes green and alive and laughing under penciled brows and darkened lashes, there stood Susan herself.

"You're just a poor little city fellow," she was saying. "Any weather makes you nervous as a kite. Who's that?" One hand, with a flash of maroon-lacquered cusps, dove into the softly moving lynx over the deep, full bosom, came out with a sparkling lorgnette, and through it Susan looked at Margaret. "No, don't tell me! Let me guess!" She came forward, stepping like a pigeon on her stilted sandals, peering down, and Margaret braced herself, her hands hard against the rough surface of the granite step, her heart beating in her palms. "It is —" (How had she forgotten that voice of Susan's, the way it made each word round and separate and charged with meaning, not the dull words that other people spoke, but sound made of feeling itself, like notes plucked softly on a violin, or like the speech of birds.) "It's Maggie! Those eyes! It is

157

Maggie!" She made a gay, grasping gesture with her hands, the lorgnette swinging on its chain. "Come up here where I can see you!"

Margaret moved up the steps, past the young man, who eyed her without curiosity, chewing his lip, impatient at the interruption; she was pinned for a moment against lynx and soft bosom, scent of perfume and powder pricking through the warm salt wet odor of the wind, Susan was kissing her with lips powdery and dry under the lipstick, her mouth had changed, the upper lip was thin and fine in spite of paint, the under lip had transverse creases in its fullness. "Darling little Maggie! This is perfect!" Susan had Margaret's cold fingers between the soft palms of her two hands. "You can stay with me while Eddie mends the car. This is an old friend, Eddie. When I was a little girl —" Susan stopped, her head a little at an angle, her lively eyes inspecting Margaret, her smile quick and sly. "Maggie was very good to me, she was lots older, but she let me tag her around, didn't you? Run along, Eddie, darling! I don't care if you never come back!"

"You'll get your fill of this before I'm back," said Eddie, firmly, and Margaret pulled her fingers out of Susan's grasp, she stood stiff, her knees quivering, she opened her mouth to speak. But Eddie, with a quick salute, was running along the driveway, the two women watching him, through the brandishing branches of trees there was a glimpse of the car, long and cream-colored and shining, pointed in from the highway. "He didn't dare drive in, this old lane is soft," said Susan. The wind carried away all sound, they saw the car back away, vanish, silent as a dream. Susan sighed. "He's crazy about that car, we practically drowned it this morning, where was it, I don't remember, the roads were rivers, just

158

rivers, Maggie! You'd never believe it. So we turned back, to try this route, and the motor began to spit. There we were, at Eastbourne. I said, Eddie, you better drive straight on to New York, I warn you! But would Eddie? No. I tell him if he'd treat a woman as he does that car!" Susan laughed. "So then I came here." Something fey leaped in her green eyes, drifted across her pointed face. "The wind shouted at me, come home, Susan, before it is too late! And here you are!"

Margaret held her hands down against the flutter of her raincoat, she said, stiffly, "I'm not older than you!"

Susan blinked at her, and then laughed. "I just said that, you know how men are! I thought you were, I really did! You *have* kept your figger, but you've let your hair go white. Um-um. Let's go inside, I can't hear in this wind, I don't like standing around, my feet are too small." She slid her hand under Margaret's arm, she trotted her along into the house, it was a dive into stillness, into an absence of buffeting which bewildered Margaret, she was a child, following Susan's bidding, all her protests, her planned upbraiding whisked away like the leaves which filled the air around the house. The hall was dim, but the drawing room had light from the long windows where the shutters had been opened, dust covers shrouded the chairs, the divan, even the crystal chandelier, everything was muted to gray, a gray film of dust over the squares of the parquetry floor, beyond the windows a film of gray, not dust, over the sky. Green-gray mildew made queer patterns, a geography of decay, over the wallpaper with its gold and satin stripes. The cool, fusty air within the house was sucked out through the opened door, the warm breath of the wind flowed in around them.

"It's a good deal like a tomb," said Susan. "But Eddie had to close the windows again, that wind would blow the paper off the wall! Maggie, it's wonderful to see you! Take that thing off your head. Your hair is pretty, just as heavy as ever, isn't it? Do you think white hair softens a face? I've wondered sometimes — but a man never likes white hair, you know, he sees that first — Ah, you're really the same Maggie, I always liked white on you, proud and quiet — You sit here by the window, I have to find something, a box of trinkets. I think I can lay my hand right on it. Then you must tell me everything you've done —"

Margaret stood there in the middle of the room where Susan left her, listening to the quick tap of heels across the hall. On the wide stairs the velvet-padded stair-runner absorbed the sound, but presently it came again overhead, little flurries of taps, like a Morse code of a search for a box of trinkets. She thought, now is my chance to say the things I've wanted to, so long; but she thought it doubtfully and in confusion, her heartbeat too rapid. So long — since anyone had called her Maggie, had, in a glance, looked past her neat and formal outer self, had — oh, however lightly, gaily! — looked at her with human warmth. It's just her voice, thought Margaret, sounding as if she cared more than she does. Look at her, decked out like a girl, traipsing about with that — that Eddie, shameless — She listened to the faint sounds overhead, she thought, I don't have to stay here, I can go on to my own house, and she wished, instead, to follow Susan upstairs, because the drawing room without her was high and gray and empty, and the air that blew in warm puffs through the open door was the breath of restlessness.

The footsteps overhead had stopped, and Margaret moved to one of the long windows. She didn't want Susan thinking she'd been struck dumb and immovable by her! The window was recessed, the blinds folded back on each side, and from the narrow, closed slats there rose a fine dust, flecks of dried enamel, circling in spirals up the window edges. I never saw wind do that, thought Margaret. Holding her hands out toward the glass, she felt it, a strong suction against the palms. A branch struck the window, startling her, leaves crumpled and torn, clung to the glass as the branch fell away. Rain had started again, fine slanting rain, which obscured the water, she was not sure whether she really saw gray waves running over the grass, well in beyond the rocky shore, as if the ocean were moving inland, or whether she saw only the rain. Even within the house now she could hear the water, loudly enough so that she was again not sure what she had heard in the hall. But she went quickly across the room. Something small and hard slid under the ball of her foot as she stepped into the hall, on the bottom step of the wide stairs was a heap of lynx fur and wine-colored coat, the hat knocked forward, hiding the face.

"Don't step on them, they're all over the place!" Susan pushed back her hat, thrust her feet out straight in front. "Damn that stair carpet!"

"Did you fall? Have you hurt yourself?" Margaret ran across to the stairs on tiptoe, skirting the small red velvet box which lay there, its cover bent open, its contents scattered. "Susan!"

"I damned near took a header." Susan hitched herself upright, she wriggled first one toe, then the other. "Don't you pull me up, not yet. Pick up that stuff for me while I get my breath." She threw aside her hat, her hair, an astonishing brick color in the dim hall, stood up over her small head in wisps and curls.

"Those heels are enough to kill anybody," said Margaret, as she bent to gather up the box and its contents.

"Nonsense." Susan drew in her feet, her skirts sliding above her knees, she laid a hand around each slim ankle. "I was hurrying, that's all. I wanted to see you before Eddie gets back."

"This is the box you had —" Margaret drew a finger over the velvet. "I remember it." White satin lining, yellowed with age, gold clasp, the cover dangling by one hinge. Most of the contents lay where the box had fallen, rings, a child's bracelet of gold, a brooch of garnets, a gold necklace with a locket, a pearl in the center of a blue enameled flower. Margaret stood erect, her temples throbbing, the necklace hanging from her finger.

"It was my first jewel case," said Susan. "I had forgotten it, it was in the little wall safe in the bedroom, the one I open with my initials. I thought there were some pearls in it. I told Eddie I'd have them made into studs." She giggled. "He's never had a dress suit, he's going to get one."

"You gave me this, once," said Margaret.

"What is it?" Susan squinted toward her. "Oh, that. How'd it get in the box, then?"

Margaret set the box on Susan's knee, she let the necklace fall into the satin bed. "You forgot to give it back."

"Did I! Oh, Maggie! And you felt bad! Oh, darling, do you want it now?"

"No." Margaret went on with her search. A string of amber had broken, the beads had rolled everywhere, at the threshold they gleamed like eyes of a cat, elsewhere they were hard to find, she gathered them cool and hard in her fingers. She found a small irregular nugget of gold,

162

and laid it in Susan's hand. Susan turned it in her painted finger-tips.

"Why, that's the very nugget Rob sent me." She looked up at Margaret, her eyes like the amber. "Your brother! His first gold, he said."

"And his last," said Margaret. Ah, it was coming, now, her chance to tell Susan —

But Susan said softly, "If he hadn't gone away!" The nugget dropped from her fingers into the box. "That always happens when I come back to this house!" She raised her voice against a gust of wind, the rain blew in across the hall. "I go soft as jelly — like an old woman! Shut the door, Maggie, we don't want to drown! And give me a hand."

Margaret tugged at the door, she edged behind it and pushed, both hands laid against the wooden panels, it seemed almost to bend, as if it would fold over her head, and then, so abruptly that she staggered and followed it for an awkward step, it was snatched away from her and whanged shut. She righted herself indignantly, disliking the large and impersonal rudeness of the day. "It must be blowing harder," she said. "I should think it had blown long enough!"

Susan laughed, a low, delighted laugh, extending her hands to Margaret.

"You never did like storms." She heaved her soft flesh up, dragging hard on Margaret's hands. "I remember. They blew up your skirts and ruffled your hair and you couldn't manage them. Pick up the box, Maggie, it's on the step there. I don't see where those pearls are, they were earrings, three little dangling pearls for each ear. Maybe I lost them."

"Yod did hurt yourself! When you fell —" Margaret felt Susan's weight pull at her shoulder, she saw the stiff dragging forward of one foot.

"I just sat down too hard. I'll be all right in a minute. Help me across to a chair, that's a good Maggie. That divan's nearer —"

Margaret got her to the divan, stood above her in dismay. But Susan leaned back, her wry mouth changing into a quick smile. "I'm too fat, I might as well admit it!"

"Where is it, Susan? Your foot? Ankle? Let me take off your shoe —"

Susan crossed one ankle over the other. "No, you don't! I'd never get it back on. Leave it alone. In ten minutes I'll be all right, I always am."

"I could run over to my house and get you something —"

"All you'd get would be a soaking! Why, look —" The two women looked, at one window and then at the other. Outside the house the rain made a solid wall, over the inner surface of the glass the rain poured, falling against the wide sill, falling against the floor, it was as if the glass had lost its essential quality and was no longer impermeable, as if the rain drove through it, piercing it like light. Margaret stared, bewilderment tasted dry in her mouth, not the sharp taste of fear.

"It must be getting in around the edges of the panes," said Susan, slowly. "That old putty —"

"I ought to wipe it up," said Margaret. "I haven't anything to wipe it up with —"

"What harm can it do?" Susan turned away from the windows, she threw her coat back from her shoulders, her throat, above the low V of the dull red frock, was white and full. "Unless it gets our feet wet. Sit down, Maggie,

164

there are so many things to say. Eddie'll be back any moment, he hates this, he'll want to get on to New York." Margaret looked again at the windows; if she watched, she would be frightened. The dust cover on the divan stretched taut from Susan's bulk to the arms, there wasn't room there. She brought one of the hooded small chairs and set it with its back toward the windows, rather near Susan, and seated herself.

"Where's your house?" asked Susan. "Near here?"

"It's the farmhouse. I bought it."

"You did?" Susan's face was alert, admiring.

"We should have gone there, instead of staying here. I've made a charming place of it, it's not like this." She glanced toward that appalling wetness. "I ought to be there now! Something might happen."

"It will be all right. Nothing can happen to your house, Maggie. You always could worry. I noticed someone lived there, someone — It's funny, your coming back here! You know, I've always thought someday I would come back. To stay. When we drive anywhere near here, I have to come. But I didn't want to stay — yet. I — I'm not happy when I'm here."

Margaret laid her hands together in her lap, her cold fingers hooked, she hugged her elbows against her sides, she felt herself spare, hard, her white dress limp now, drabbled, and anger began to shrill in her head, like the highest note in which the wind now spoke, anger at the difference between herself and this soft woman on the couch, a heap of silk and furs and jewels, her painted mouth beguiling Margaret with her Maggie this and that.

"You see" — again that fey look, a shadow over Susan's gaiety — "I'll tell you — it was strange, my landing here just today. Yes, I'll tell you. Did you wonder why we were so crazy, driving to New York in such

165

weather? You'd never guess. Eddie's going to school, he's going to be an engineer, he's not really a chauffeur. But he's very proud, he didn't want me to help him at first. And I thought I'd like to settle down, I'd like to be sure I had somebody. We were going to get married. I haven't been married for a long time. He's younger, but he's quite old for his years, he's always had to look out for himself." She lifted her lorgnette, it shimmered in unsteady fingers as she held it to her eyes. "Aren't you ever afraid of being alone? When you get older, you don't want to be alone. But the minute I stepped in this house, I knew. I'd be lonelier with him — Who lives in your house with you?"

"I am alone," said Margaret. Her anger was a rod now, stiffening her back. "But thank God, I'm respectable!"

Susan blinked through her lorgnette, she let it fly down against her full bosom, she tipped back her head with its ragged petals of hair, and laughed. "Oh, Maggie! Maggie, darling!" Her laughter was warm and round in the strange gray room. "What good does that do you?"

"You wouldn't understand, you're shameless and dreadful, your name is a byword, men leer after you —" Margaret had to stop, her anger was a tight band around her chest, her heart strained madly against it.

Susan stopped laughing, she leaned forward a little, holding out her hands, fingers spread, soft white palms with deep creases turned up, as if she held Margaret's words away from her ears. "Why, Maggie, you — you don't like me?" Her eyes were incredulous, her mouth sagged a trifle.

Margaret stumbled to her feet, she pushed away the chair, and before she could make a word in her parched throat the hall door crashed open, wind tore into the house, bellying the covers on the furniture, and with it

166

the boy Sam, water running from his cap, from his yellow slicker, so that he stood in a pool there at the entrance to the drawing room.

"Geeze!" His voice was faint, a gasp, and gathered force as he caught his breath. "Hurry up! Eddie sent me — I had to leave the car — they's a tree down — you'll have to walk out to it — Come along, I say! We ain't got a minute!"

Susan looked at him, she tucked her feet further under the edge of the couch. "Where's Eddie?" she asked.

"Working on your car, him and Bill. Water in the base." His sandy face was blanched with rain and excitement, he wriggled inside his slicker, wanting to be off. "You gotta hustle, I tell you! Geeze, I never seen nothing like it! The tide didn't go down, Bill says when it's high tide again, the road'll be under water, we got an hour to make it."

"Where's the car?" asked Margaret. "Can't you bring it —"

"I can't climb over a tree with it!" Sam shrieked above the wind, he swung his arms. "Can't you get a move on you? You can walk a few steps, can't you?"

Margaret listened. There was a new note in the wind, one she had never heard before in all her life, a strange, shrill, high note: it hurt her eardrums, it went spinning into hollow places under her skull, almost obscenely, a note beyond the range of hearing. She scurried across the room toward Sam, picking up her raincoat, thrusting her arms into the sleeves.

"Come on, you!" yelled Sam, jerking his hand at Susan.

Margaret's fingers were clumsy, tying the scarf over her head, she stood at the doorway, the rain struck her face, she drew one long breath, and held it,

167

aching-endlessly, dashing a hand against her wet eyelids that she might see. One of the two great elms which stood each side of the porte-cochere, the one farther from the house, toward the road, without a sound that she could hear above the wind, with slow and appalling dignity, swayed, bent, twisted its leafy bulk as if it turned to look at the enemy that struck it down, and fell, carrying with it a great round slab of yellowish earth, a mat of roots and wet soil as high as the roof of the carriage entrance. Sam whimpered with excitement.

"Now you see! My God, ain't this something! Get her started, will you?"

Margaret heard Susan's voice, it made a quiet place in all this tumult, for a moment she did not hear the separate words, speech seemed to have no meaning, she had to shape them again in her own throat before she understood what Susan had said. "I won't stir a step in this downpour. I'd be drenched to the skin."

Sam seized Margaret's wrist, jerked it. His young mouth twisted in grotesque attempt to be strong and male, rescuing women. "I can't drag her," he cried. "We gotta go, you come, Miss Turner, you ain't such a fool!"

Margaret dragged her raincoat together with her free hand, for an instant she felt herself plunge forward with the boy, his strength running beside her, carrying her to safety. Then she wrenched her wrist out of his grasp and took a quick step toward the drawing room, and her voice was strange in her ears as she cried out, "Susan —"

Susan waved her hand, a careless farewell, she pushed herself to her feet, her coat sliding in a soft mound around her on the floor, her face impertinent, mocking.

Swifter than thought, Margaret knew. "Run along, Sammy." She made her stiff face smile. "Tell — tell Eddie we're all right here. Tell him Mrs. Field can't —"

168

"Run along yourself, Maggie! What you waiting for?" Susan was imperative, silencing her. "I don't want your company! You're too respectable! The house won't blow down."

Margaret pushed at Sam, who hung in the doorway, tormented. "For Heaven's sake, Sam, get out! I don't intend to drown myself in that rain! Why should I want to go to town? Pull that door shut after you —" She laid herself against the door, his desire to be off and her will together shut it, and water curled swiftly under it, over the floor.

She hesitated, taking a few steps into the drawing room. Susan had dropped back on the couch, she was pulling her coat from under her feet, her eyes angry, green, as she looked at Margaret.

"You're a fool, Maggie!"

"You can't even stand on that foot, can you?"

"What's that to do with you?"

"Why didn't you let me tell him?" Margaret moved nearer, step by step, her hands twisting together at her breast. "Were you afraid your Eddie would risk his life, trying to get you?"

Susan laid her coat over her knees, her hands smoothing the fur, the fingers disappearing in the long tawny hairs, she was silent a moment; when she looked up her face was somber, on each side of her mouth lower than the rouged cheek-bones was a dull red streak. "No, Maggie. If you must know, I was afraid he wouldn't. I'd rather not know. Think how embarrassed I'd be if I called for help — and no one came! This way —" She turned her head, listening; the arrows of the wind whistled over the house. "There's a queer smell to the air," she said. "It's like some strange drug, you take a sniff and you don't go on fooling yourself." Her somberness was gone, in a little

169

flashing smile. "Why did you stay, Maggie? You're scared to death, you know you are, that nice boy would have taken you —"

"Let me see your foot, Susan Lathrop," said Margaret, sternly. She knelt stiffly in front of Susan, she pushed the folds of coat away from Susan's knees, and laid her hands on the pointed toes of the sandals, pulling both feet toward her. Then she sat back, her fingers touching the swollen ankle, puffy and discolored through the chiffon stocking. "Your poor foot!" she said. Susan leaned forward, eyeing both extended feet. "I have such nice ankles, too," she said, gaily. Then, "Why, Maggie! You're crying!"

"You would have stayed here —"

Susan stretched one hand out, pushed the scarf back from Margaret's hair, smoothed the hair softly, and laughed. "And so you stayed. With a shameless, dreadful — Maggie, what do people say about me?" Her fingertip touched Margaret's forehead, brushed over her eyelids.

Margaret got to her feet, with an abrupt movement. The iron band, the iron rod of her anger had gone, she did not know what the feeling was which inundated her, it was like the rain, finding its way past barriers of glass and wood, it was like the wave curling over grass, receding, advancing again.

"It's not raining so hard," she said. "Look, it's stopping!" The wind had no shrillness now, through the window they could see the water, breaking in long streamers of white. "I'm going to run over to my house, to get some things for that ankle. It's just a little way."

Susan reached for her skirt, but Margaret moved with her quick, light step toward the hall. "Don't go, Maggie! Suppose you couldn't get back!"

170

"I'll get back!" Margaret chose the one argument to silence Susan. "I ought to see that everything's all right in my house, if the rain got in there —"

"Leave the door open," called Susan. "It's too warm —"

The door opened so readily, swinging inward, that Margaret thought someone must stand there, someone who had come for them, Sam, or Eddie. No one. There was a yellow lake where the elm tree had torn up the great slab of soil, with a ragged fringe of turf, and water rippled along the driveway. But the rain had stopped; the mist which filled the air was salty on her mouth. She would get her feet soaked, but it was so warm she wouldn't catch cold; she could get bandage stuff, rubbing alcohol, perhaps pack a basket with food, it might be several hours before anyone could reach the house. The water was only ankle-deep, she splashed ahead, had the wind changed? It seemed running to meet her, in warm little puffs, coming over the land. She rounded the rear corner of the house and stopped. Ahead of her rose a great mass of green, a tree, hiding the sky, filling the space ahead of her; she thought, amazed, why that's the way a bird sees a tree, looking into it, and then, hastily, moved out around its bulk, her feet heavy in the tangled grass and sodden ground. It was a long way past a fallen tree, its roots stood up above her, she could not tell just where she had come, and she stopped. Something was wrong, like looking at a familiar face and finding it had no eyes, no mouth — The barns! Where were they? She began to run, laboring, her breath catching, there were other trees down, but already her eyes had accustomed themselves to that form of disaster, she could see ahead of her under the mottled sky the rising land on which her house stood, she could see the house itself, its white paint shining, the only clear

171

tone in all the landscape; it had been built to weather storms, she thought, its low, sturdy shape settled against the land. The old apple tree at one side sprawled askew. Margaret stumbled against something, a log, no, a timber, gray, with marks of the ax like ripples of water, a beam from the barn. The water was deeper here, halfway to her knees, and ahead of her, ridiculously, as if it walked over the field, moved a splintered door, she could see the hasp where a padlock had hung. She took another step, and stopped, trembling.

The door was floating more quickly now, oscillating. Those green clumps must be the tops of the lilac bushes, and lilacs stood higher than her head. If she hurried, plunging forward, she could still cross. She stared, turning her head slowly in a half circle. The ocean was moving inland, breaking through at the low bit of shingle where the wall of rocks began to merge into the long sandy beach, cutting across, gouging across, the sod under her feet broke under her weight, eaten by the water, and she braced herself, feeling water move against her legs. The thought of her house was a voice shouting at her, hurry, you can still reach me! Safety, shelter, her house, in a way her life, her love, all that she had! She was strong, the current could not yet be swift, she could swim. The muddy water eddied around the lilac clumps, she saw it close over one of them. She could reach her house, and stay there, she could not return. What claim had Susan on her, like that of her house? *Don't go, Maggie!* She set her teeth into her lower lip, she thought, in a kind of dull incredulity, Why, no tide ever rose as fast as this, and slowly, without another glance at water, hill, or house, she turned back. As she went she thought the water followed at her heels, and when at last she reached the stone steps she was not surprised that the pool beneath the elm-tree roots had merged into a larger flood, and that little waves beat up against the disk of mud. We're on an island, now. Cut off.

Her side hurt, and she stood, pressing her hand against it, before she went into the house. She closed the door, and the squelch of her shoes was loud in what seemed, after the outer tumult, like silence. Susan was sitting just where Margaret had left her, and her breast rose and fell in one long sigh. Margaret hung her raincoat over the newel post, she rubbed a handkerchief over her face, her eyes burned; she wrung the bottom of her skirt, and tried to pat it smooth.

"I couldn't get anything for your ankle," she said. "It was so wet —"

Susan beckoned her nearer. "Are you all right? I thought once I heard you cry out! I started after you, but I can't hop on one foot. Not far. I told you you'd just get drenched. You — you didn't see anyone — coming?"

"No, I didn't." Margaret sank down on the chair, she couldn't yet draw a full breath, her toes curled inside her wet shoes. Irritation jingled through her weariness. How could anybody come? She opened her mouth to tell Susan what she had seen, and said, instead, "Does it hurt much?"

"It hurt like hell while you were gone." Susan grimaced. "You know, the way everything's worse when you're by yourself. Wind, rain, aches, anything. I don't mind it now. I tell you, if I stuck it up —" She swung around sidewise on the divan, and with both hands under her plump knee, hoisted it up. A scarlet garter made a cushion of the soft flesh above the knee. Susan patted it, hoisted the other leg, and leaned back against the arm of the divan. "That's better. Now you pull your chair

173

around, and we'll talk. I think the storm is over, the sky is lighter, see?"

Lighter, yes, with a sullen yellowish tinge under the dull clouds. Susan held one wrist near her eyes, squinting at the tiny jeweled watch, the sleeve slipping back from the plump white arm, creased at the wrist like a baby's. "It's stopped," she said. "I must have hit it when I took that tumble. Now we don't even know what time it is!" She eased herself a little into place, her hands looked small, lying against the maroon silk which strained over her wide soft thighs. "Well, I never did know the time! You always did, Maggie! Remember how it worried you, being on time?" She laughed. "Well, we've no date to keep today, have we? It's nice, having you here. It took a storm, didn't it, to make you put up with me?" Her smile was sly. "You don't really think I'm all those names you were calling me, do you? Anyway, you stayed with me. You know, when you started for your house, I thought maybe you were clearing out."

Margaret hitched her chair over the floor, nearer the couch. "I wanted to," she said, her mouth grim. "I don't know why I came back." She thought, all these things are true about Susan, disgraceful, disgusting, and yet I'm sitting here — I don't mind being wet, or frightened — She lifted her head as the whole house shivered, she heard the wind after it had passed the house, and then a rumbling clatter, an avalanche of dull noise.

"Is it raining stones now?" said Susan.

"I know. The chimney!" Margaret glanced behind her at the marble and onyx face of the fireplace, she thought the sheet of metal which covered the opening bulged outward, she saw a dark lip of sooty water along the lower edge, creeping out over the hearth.

174

"What's a chimney more or less?" Susan relaxed again, but she laid a hand on Margaret's knee. "I was thinking — while you were gone — that's what this damned house always does to me, sets me thinking. You never married, Maggie? Have you been happy?"

Margaret sat very still, the queer sweet smell of the air perplexed her, it was like morning, not like any morning she had known, but some morning in a dream. She tried to gather around her the tatters of the Margaret Turner she had meant to show to Susan, to confound Susan, a proud, righteous, worthy woman, and she couldn't find even a tatter.

"You should have married Lester Field," said Susan. "If he'd had you admiring him, looking up to him — if he'd had to work —"

"But you took him, you ruined him."

"You might have put up a fight for him. I didn't know he'd ever seen you! Oh, I heard, afterwards. He was a snob, Maggie, a lazy, selfish snob. You were the farmer's daughter, and do you know what I was? I was a good marriage. Making a good marriage and sleeping with it aren't the same thing! I was glad when he took that header off his horse, it takes too long to die of drink. When I come back here I think about him — and Robert. It's funny, isn't it, how you see the ends of stories, as you grow older. When you're young, you never think that anything will end, you will love forever, you'll suffer forever, you're sewed up tight in what you feel right now —" Her mouth trembled a little, the lipstick on the under lip had smeared thin, leaving a fine line of red below the outline of the lip. "Now I know all the endings. I know how things come out. Oh, I pretend I don't, that's the only way to have any fun —" Her fingers pressed on Margaret's knee, and the two looked steadily at each

175

other — are you frightened, uneasy? — as the whole house strained under the wind, timbers sliding behind plaster, like the sound of movement in wood and metal of a ship.

It's true, thought Margaret; you begin to see the pattern that a whole life makes, you do know the ends of stories. I have been troubled about my own, it was coming in a circle back to all its beginnings. She laid one hand over Susan's, she felt a lightness in her blood, an ease, it was like a dream to sit there, with hatred and envy gone.

"Look," said Susan, "it is raining again." She turned to glance over the back of the divan toward the windows, they saw the way the water had covered the floor, running under the door, down from the window ledges, out from the fireplace, until it made a streaked covering, reflecting oddly the shapes of the chairs, the angle of the walls, reaching the carved feet of the divan.

"If you could walk —" Margaret was bewildered. "Could you get upstairs, if I helped?"

"I can't, not without crawling." Susan lifted her coat away from the floor. "I'm comfortable right here. You aren't scared, Maggie? Rain can't wash this house away."

"I don't know what I am," said Margaret, a little pettishly.

"I must look a sight," said Susan. "Where's my handbag? I had it when we came in. There it is, on the mantel, get it for me, Maggie, dear."

Margaret took the few steps to the mantel, she thought the tesselated floor moved under her feet, she thought as she looked down that water crept up along the lines of the patterned oak, how could it? Was there a new sound in the house, a gurgle of water under the floor, a steady slap-slap?

176

"You know, Eddie reminds me a lot of Robert," Susan was saying, as Margaret handed her the bag. She poked a finger under the rhinestone clasp and spread the bag open. "I hadn't thought of it before. What happened to Robert, Maggie?"

"He died. He got typhoid in that mining camp." (Where he went because of you: tell her!) Margaret stood close to the couch.

"Dead?" Susan looked up, a vanity case snapped open in one hand. "I didn't know." There was a crease between her plucked, accented brows. "He would be an old man now, wouldn't he? He was older than you — or me — I never thought of that before." She shrugged. "I don't like elderly men, they fuss so — diet, liver — they have hairs in their ears and their teeth clack! Robert — ah, he didn't have to grow old! He was beautiful. Eddie isn't really like him. Why, I remember the row they made about Robert, right here in this room! Father and Mother — about Susan Lathrop and her groom! I didn't care, I loved him. But he cared, he was furious. He went away, west. I would have waited forever — at least I thought so." She began to pat powder over her face, the scent strong for a moment. "But I couldn't stand his taking the money."

"What money?" Margaret leaned closer, her hands clasped; Susan's voice had dropped; it was an unhappy whisper against the background of steady noise around them. Susan set her lips together and dusted her chin. "What money?" urged Margaret.

"The money my father gave him, if he'd go off. I — I suppose he was poor —"

"Is that what they told you?" Margaret's scorn brought Susan's eyes up from the mirror. "You might have known it was a lie! Robert never took a cent, except

177

his wages. Why, I sent him money that year, when I began to teach, money for food!"

"I might have known," said Susan, slowly. "I wasn't as smart then. Why, Maggie, it's like a present! Everything was criss-cross, and we're laying it all straight!"

"When he died, his landlady sent me his things," said Margaret. "His account book, and a picture of you — and a letter. I would never give you the letter."

"I don't want to see the picture!" Susan peered again into the little mirror, she fished a lipstick out of the bag. She made a stroke with the pencil, but her hand wavered, and the crimson was a clown's mouth. Angrily she dabbed at it with a handkerchief, sticking out the point of her tongue to moisten a corner. "I don't care how I look," she said. She dropped the lipstick, mirror, handkerchief, into the purse, and pinched the rhinestones shut. "I've been a fool, haven't I? But you have to have somebody to love as long as you live, don't you?" Her voice was warm again, and clear. "Whatever they've been, I've had the loving of them. Nobody can take that away!"

Margaret had drawn away from the divan, her shoulders hunched, her hands doubled into fists. She wanted to listen to Susan, but something, *something* was moving past the windows at the end of the room, was looking in. She walked toward the windows, slowly, not to frighten Susan, her feet slipping in the water, inches deep, which covered the floor, not quiet water, but water that swung as if the whole house rocked a little. The room was darker, and she saw she stared at the peaked roof of a house outside the windows, cutting off all light, all glimpse of ocean, a jagged hole where there had been a chimney; and it floated higher than the upper ledges of the windows. Margaret looked at it without great

178

concern; she had lost her standard by which she measured what happened, nothing now was astonishing. The dark, slanting roof moved toward the house, as if it meant to climb in through the windows, and then was sucked away. Margaret saw the ocean, it had come above the window sills, a wave climbed up the sash, and its spray stung her face there inside the house. She looked out, across the gray-green rollers, not surprised that all the land was gone, every tree was gone, and the house itself was islanded. She saw, between her and the sky, one great wall, like fog turned into solid matter, high as the sky, advancing without haste, with dignity. When that breaks, she thought, and turned away from the window. She could run, she could climb the stairs, the attic of the house was high, she would be safe there!

"What you looking at?" asked Susan.

"A wave," said Margaret. She started across the floor, her feet begged her to run, they were separate, alive, insisting upon flight, she couldn't save Susan, too, there was no time — no time. At the edge of the couch she stopped, her hand reached for Susan's, she slipped to the floor, shutting her eyes, laying her face against Susan's soft breast. "Hang on," she whispered, "hang on tight to me! I'm not afraid any more, with you."

"Why, Maggie!" said Susan, and under Margaret's ear her heart, undefeated, quickened its beat. For an instant, in the great blackness which filled the room, a whirling blackness under the wall of water, Margaret thought that they were children again, running ahead of the storm, she with her hand in Susan's. "We'll stick together!" cried Susan, and her voice had the golden curl of a trumpet. "Till we die!" If it was fear that Margaret felt, it had, at the last, the strong sweet taste of great elation.

Mabel L. Robinson and Helen R. Hull in front of their Maine
house, late 1950s.

Afterword

Helen Hull (1888–1971) began publishing short stories and one-act plays around 1914, her work first appearing in *The Woman's Journal* (a suffrage magazine) and the leftist *Masses,* as well as in more mainstream publications such as *Century* and *Harper's* and "little" magazines such as *Seven Arts* and *Touchstone.* All of the stories in this collection except *Last September* are among her early work, written around the time of World War I.

In 1914, Hull and her life-long companion Mabel Louise Robinson (1878?–1962) began spending their summers in North Brooklin, Maine, along with a small group of women from New

York, most of them part of literary, artistic, or political circles. They brought with them from the city and, some of them, from earlier days at Wellesley College, their belief in a world of new possibilities for women. Their penchant for racing along country roads on their bicycles, wearing middy blouses and knickers, earned them the local nickname "the Bicycle Girls."

Their writing, their cycling, and their commitment to each other and to freedom from traditional female roles were indeed unconventional at a time when women still could not vote in the United States and the "Woman Question" (e.g., Should middle-class women work outside the home? Should women be educated?) was a topic of hot debate throughout the country. Even today, Hull and Robinson's Maine neighbors remember them from that period — not altogether favorably — as "strong-minded" and "independent."

While the neighbors may have frowned on the presence of those qualities in women, Hull clearly prized them. In the first six stories in this volume — the "Cynthia" stories — Hull describes a part of the growth process toward strength and independence. Hull's heroines struggle to achieve knowledge, self-possession, and a more accurate vision of reality and of possibility. They learn that, in order to grow into knowledge and self-possession, they must be strong, wary, clever, determined, disobedient, isolated, and silent — hardly the set of characteristics usually associated with "good" daughters or mothers.

The "Cynthia" stories are concerned with what it means for a female to grow up in middle-class America. Hull suggests that women who follow the traditional prescriptions for female behavior are forced by cultural definitions of wifedom and motherhood to remain immature, not fully developed human beings. This is reinforced in two of her early novels, *Quest* (Macmillan, 1922) and *The Surry Family* (Macmillan, 1925), for which the "Cynthia" stories were embryos.

Hull describes the constant interplay between what the young women manage to learn for themselves about growth and what is expected of them as wives- and mothers-in-training.

182

Cynthia's desire for independence constantly conflicts with a social mandate to mature by growing into new forms of dependence and subservience. By observing her mothers and other adult women and by listening to what she is told about "proper" behavior, Cynthia becomes initiated into knowledge of gender systems; she begins to see what she will have to pay for being a woman. We see in these stories a heroine at a moment of discovery and commitment, encouraged by the fact that she has gained some valuable insight and determined to get on with her life as best she can.

In "The Fire" (*Century*, November 1917), Mrs. Bates exacts her daughter Cynthia's obedience but loses her loyalty.

It is the art teacher, Miss Egert, who represents for Cynthia a world of possibility, a world larger than that in which her parents would confine her: one which is spacious enough to contain beauty, art, purposeful work, and, above all, a joy in life that enables Miss Egert to see in paintings swiftness and gladness, a passionate vision that prompts her to delight, in the dancing flames of a bonfire.

It is when Miss Egert's "soft, pale lips . . . tremble against the girl's mouth" as she urges Cynthia to "keep searching" that Cynthia feels ecstatic. She knows that she is pledging herself to a mystery "which trembled all about her," and what has just been literally trembling against her is Miss Egert's kiss. Because this scene at the bonfire is so emotionally charged for Cynthia, Hull seems to suggest that she will eventually form powerful, perhaps erotic, attachments to other women — as one part of the larger new world she seeks.

The intensity of Mrs. Bates's anger at Cynthia's growing attachment to Miss Egert is a sign of the growing social awareness, fear, and condemnation of homosexuality in the early part of this century, fueled by the popularizing of the work of men such as Freud, Krafft-Ebing, and Havelock Ellis. The "Cynthia" stories mark an interesting transition in the process Lillian Faderman describes (*Surpassing the Love of Men* 1981): Around the time of World War I, magazine fiction shifts from unself-conscious portrayal of passionate friendships between women to silence or outright condemnation. In "The Fire," Hull takes the woman accused of what had come to be considered perverse or unhealthy behavior in the view of the professional "sexologists" and presents her instead as the responsible, unselfish, and admirable adult worthy of emulation; on the other hand, the socially-sanctioned, "healthy" mother who voices the growing popular and professional hysteria about lesbianism is childish, unloving, and cruel. The adolescent girl, meanwhile, remains oblivious to the nature of the suspicion underlying her mother's anger. Hull presents Cynthia's love for Miss Egert as a saving grace; her maturing means that she will leave the restricted world of her mother, taking with her Miss Egert's values and the memory of her love.

Published in 1920 in Mary Fanton Roberts's little magazine *Touchstone*, "Separation provides a counterpoint to "The Fire." While Cynthia of "The Fire" tries to bring into focus some vision of her future, this Cynthia works to see her present reality accurately, first casting off romantic illusion and then coming into knowledge of her power. For this Cynthia, the meaning of power is the ability to defend oneself against adult intrusion, and the skills she is developing to secure and maintain this power include wariness, cleverness, vigilance, clear-sightedness, and silence.

As in "The Fire," here the awareness of sexual "irregularity" has not yet filtered down to the adolescent Cynthia. The mother, however, uses homophobic accusations to reassert her control and to mask her own pain and frustration. She is remarkably inarticulate on the subject, and Hull counts on an audience alert to references to homosexuality to fill in what Cynthia does not understand and what Mrs. Moore can only manage to allude to in classic lines such as, "I won't have her suspecting me of — of all sorts of things!"

As in "The Fire," Hull does not criticize her adolescent protagonist for loving women. Cynthia is shown to be immature not for loving a woman but for admiring one unworthy of her respect; what she outgrows is her naivete. She does not achieve maturity by substituting men for women in her daydreams;

184

rather, she stops daydreaming altogether. Growth for her means an almost literal self-possession: at the end she holds herself in her own arms and knows that she can protect herself.

The point of conflict between Cynthia and her mother in "Alley Ways" (*Century*, February 1918) is again the daughter's friendship with someone "inappropriate," this time a working-class contemporary.

Cynthia develops class consciousness and a growing sense of the complexity of moral issues.

Like "The Fire" and "Separation," "Alley Ways" is remarkable because Hull does *not* define growth for the adolescent girl as abandoning homoeroticism in favor of heterosexuality. Cynthia's erotic response to Rachel is presented as intense and beautiful. What becomes increasingly unappealing to Cynthia is married middle-class heterosexuality.

"Alley Ways" presents the pain of a young woman whose female friend, with whom she has had a passionate friendship, leaves her behind for marriage. In another sense, however, it is Cynthia who leaves Rachel behind as she grows into moral knowledge and class-consciousness. "Alley Ways" records an adolescent's struggle with ethical issues through a process of disillusionment with her friend, her parents, and their middle-class world. Rachel becomes an inappropriate object for Cynthia's affection not because she is female but because she is insensitive and her thinking is class-bound. In the end, Cynthia loses both Queenie and Rachel. What she has in their stead is a commitment to a quest that is exciting but also confusing, frightening, and isolating.

Published in *Seven Arts* in February 1917, "Groping" is a story about sexual confusion.

Reading this story today, we tend to think of Cynthia as younger than her 17 or so years, largely because of the changes in U.S. sexual mores.

Cynthia has four potential sources of knowledge: her mother, her friend Mary, social/religious convention, and her own experience.

Hull portrays Cynthia here, as in the other stories, as an adolescent who is unaware that others may expect her to recoil from passionate responses to or from other women.

The reader is left with a sense of her potential: her energy, the intensity of her erotic response, her dawning knowledge that what she has been taught about "love" (whether the term means emotion, eroticism, or the appeal of potential marriage partners) is not necessarily accurate.

Published in *Touchstone* in August 1918, "Discovery" presents the same Cynthia several years later, more knowledgeable, experienced. She has achieved perspective, a distance which enables her, in encounters with three different people, to act effectively in her own interest. In each case, she exercises power and finds the experience quite gratifying.

She understands more clearly what the boundaries of her world have been, and she is determined to embark on a life of activity rather than passivity, of self-determination rather than social prescription.

Cynthia of "The Fusing" (*Touchstone*, July 1919) runs up against familiar problems. This Cynthia finally is able to identify her insecurity and her unconscious search for contained, structured worlds (e.g., academia), for "something outside to hold her, cradle her." By the end of "The Fusing," she pulls her fear into the open and believes that she can now move ahead, knowing that the real source of her strength lies not outside but within her.

In "Last September," Margaret Turner, a woman much older than any of the Cynthias, is still "opening out"; in this case, however, she does so as her world is closing in: she is in dire economic straits, she is old, and the natural world (in the form of a hurricane) is about to crush her.

Unlike D. H. Lawrence in his novella *The Fox*, in which he dispatches one of a pair of devoted women into marriage and kills off the other with a falling tree, Hull makes her characters stay alive until they can be reunited, sort out the differences between them, and end their lives in each other's arms. It seems ironic today that Hull's novella was originally published in *Good*

Housekeeping, a very traditional magazine. We can probably thank agism — along with Hull's solid professional reputation as a literary authority on American family life — for the editors' being oblivious to the erotic power of the story — and hence allowing it to get into print.

Although *Last September* appeared first as a short story in *Good Housekeeping* (July 1939), the version that appears in this volume is basically what Hull published in 1940 under the title *With the One Coin for Fee* in her collection of four novellas called *Experiment.* We have retained the title *Last September* from *Good Housekeeping,* but the text here restores the full, original version, as published in *Experiment.* In cutting some 40% from Hull's manuscript, the editors of *Good Housekeeping* dropped many of the flashbacks that are crucial to establishing Margaret's and Susan's characters. In addition, the *GH* editors "normalized" the punctuation to create shorter sentences rather than the comma-spliced units Hull used to convey the way Margaret thinks. Consequently, the deliberately fluid style was altered in *GH* to a more pedestrian, less "stream-of-consciousness" mode.

The one departure in this text from the *Experiment* version is the conclusion, which here omits a final sentence that Hull added to the original for that collection, apparently in order to make it clear that Margaret and Susan are indeed killed in the hurricane. Since that point seems clear enough, this edition closes with the ending which leaves Margaret in "great elation" and provides the most appropriate emotional closure to the story. The sentence which concludes the *Experiment* version reads: "The wave walked over the house, the wind pried at the walls, the front wall yielded first, falling outward, with a soughing soft note, and the water swept through" (New York: Coward-McCann, 1940, p. 67).

These brief notes on *Last September* do not begin to convey either the strength or the delicacy of this story, possibly Hull's finest piece. She presents Margaret and Susan with remarkable understanding and compassion in a story beautifully crafted.

Last September does indeed deserve, as *New York Times* reviewer Rose Feld said in 1940, to stand as a classic.

A few of the publications of
THE NAIAD PRESS, INC.
P.O. Box 10543 ● Tallahassee, Florida 32302
Phone (904) 539-9322
Mail orders welcome. Please include 15% postage.

CHERISHED LOVE by Evelyn Kennedy. 192 pp. Erotic
Lesbian love story.   ISBN 0-941483-08-8 $8.95

LAST SEPTEMBER by Helen R. Hull. 208 pp. Six stories & a
glorious novella.   ISBN 0-941483-09-6   8.95

THE SECRET IN THE BIRD by Camarin Grae. 312 pp. Striking,
psychological suspense novel.   ISBN 0-941483-05-3   8.95

TO THE LIGHTNING by Catherine Ennis. 208 pp. Romantic
Lesbian 'Robinson Crusoe' adventure.   ISBN 0-941483-06-1   8.95

THE OTHER SIDE OF VENUS by Shirley Verel. 224 pp.
Luminous, romantic love story.   ISBN 0-941483-07-X   8.95

DREAMS AND SWORDS by Katherine V. Forrest. 192 pp.
Romantic, erotic, imaginative stories.   ISBN 0-941483-03-7   8.95

MEMORY BOARD by Jane Rule. 336 pp. Memorable novel
about an aging Lesbian couple.   ISBN 0-941483-02-9   8.95

THE ALWAYS ANONYMOUS BEAST by Lauren Wright
Douglas. 224 pp. A Caitlin Reese mystery. First in a series.
                                             ISBN 0-941483-04-5   8.95

SEARCHING FOR SPRING by Patricia A. Murphy. 224 pp.
Novel about the recovery of love.   ISBN 0-941483-00-2   8.95

DUSTY'S QUEEN OF HEARTS DINER by Lee Lynch. 240 pp.
Romantic blue-collar novel.   ISBN 0-941483-01-0   8.95

PARENTS MATTER by Ann Muller. 240 pp. Parents'
relationships with Lesbian daughters and gay sons.
                                             ISBN 0-930044-91-6   9.95

THE PEARLS by Shelley Smith. 176 pp. Passion and fun in
the Caribbean sun.   ISBN 0-930044-93-2   7.95

MAGDALENA by Sarah Aldridge. 352 pp. Epic Lesbian novel
set on three continents.   ISBN 0-930044-99-1   8.95

THE BLACK AND WHITE OF IT by Ann Allen Shockley.
144 pp. Short stories.   ISBN 0-930044-96-7   7.95

SAY JESUS AND COME TO ME by Ann Allen Shockley. 288
pp. Contemporary romance.   ISBN 0-930044-98-3   8.95

LOVING HER by Ann Allen Shockley. 192 pp. Romantic love
story.   ISBN 0-930044-97-5   7.95

MURDER AT THE NIGHTWOOD BAR by Katherine V.
Forrest. 240 pp. A Kate Delafield mystery. Second in a series.
ISBN 0-930044-92-4   8.95

ZOE'S BOOK by Gail Pass. 224 pp. Passionate, obsessive love
story.   ISBN 0-930044-95-9   7.95

WINGED DANCER by Camarin Grae. 228 pp. Erotic Lesbian
adventure story.   ISBN 0-930044-88-6   8.95

PAZ by Camarin Grae. 336 pp. Romantic Lesbian adventurer
with the power to change the world.   ISBN 0-930044-89-4   8.95

SOUL SNATCHER by Camarin Grae. 224 pp. A puzzle, an
adventure, a mystery — Lesbian romance.   ISBN 0-930044-90-8   8.95

THE LOVE OF GOOD WOMEN by Isabel Miller. 224 pp.
Long-awaited new novel by the author of the beloved *Patience
and Sarah*.   ISBN 0-930044-81-9   8.95

THE HOUSE AT PELHAM FALLS by Brenda Weathers. 240
pp. Suspenseful Lesbian ghost story.   ISBN 0-930044-79-7   7.95

HOME IN YOUR HANDS by Lee Lynch. 240 pp. More stories
from the author of *Old Dyke Tales*.   ISBN 0-930044-80-0   7.95

EACH HAND A MAP by Anita Skeen. 112 pp. Real-life poems
that touch us all.   ISBN 0-930044-82-7   6.95

SURPLUS by Sylvia Stevenson. 342 pp. A classic early Lesbian
novel.   ISBN 0-930044-78-9   6.95

PEMBROKE PARK by Michelle Martin. 256 pp. Derring-do
and daring romance in Regency England.   ISBN 0-930044-77-0   7.95

THE LONG TRAIL by Penny Hayes. 248 pp. Vivid adventures
of two women in love in the old west.   ISBN 0-930044-76-2   8.95

HORIZON OF THE HEART by Shelley Smith. 192 pp. Hot
romance in summertime New England.   ISBN 0-930044-75-4   7.95

AN EMERGENCE OF GREEN by Katherine V. Forrest. 288
pp. Powerful novel of sexual discovery.   ISBN 0-930044-69-X   8.95

THE LESBIAN PERIODICALS INDEX edited by Claire
Potter. 432 pp. Author & subject index.   ISBN 0-930044-74-6   29.95

DESERT OF THE HEART by Jane Rule. 224 pp. A classic;
basis for the movie *Desert Hearts*.   ISBN 0-930044-73-8   7.95

SPRING FORWARD/FALL BACK by Sheila Ortiz Taylor.
288 pp. Literary novel of timeless love.   ISBN 0-930044-70-3   7.95

FOR KEEPS by Elisabeth Nonas. 144 pp. Contemporary novel
about losing and finding love.   ISBN 0-930044-71-1   7.95

TORCHLIGHT TO VALHALLA by Gale Wilhelm. 128 pp.
Classic novel by a great Lesbian writer.   ISBN 0-930044-68-1   7.95

LESBIAN NUNS: BREAKING SILENCE edited by Rosemary
Curb and Nancy Manahan. 432 pp. Unprecedented autobiographies
of religious life.   ISBN 0-930044-62-2   9.95

THE SWASHBUCKLER by Lee Lynch. 288 pp. Colorful novel
set in Greenwich Village in the sixties.   ISBN 0-930044-66-5   7.95

MISFORTUNE'S FRIEND by Sarah Aldridge. 320 pp. Histori-
cal Lesbian novel set on two continents.   ISBN 0-930044-67-3   7.95

A STUDIO OF ONE'S OWN by Ann Stokes. Edited by
Dolores Klaich. 128 pp. Autobiography.   ISBN 0-930044-64-9   7.95

SEX VARIANT WOMEN IN LITERATURE by Jeannette
Howard Foster. 448 pp. Literary history.   ISBN 0-930044-65-7   8.95

A HOT-EYED MODERATE by Jane Rule. 252 pp. Hard-hitting
essays on gay life; writing; art.   ISBN 0-930044-57-6   7.95

INLAND PASSAGE AND OTHER STORIES by Jane Rule.
288 pp. Wide-ranging new collection.   ISBN 0-930044-56-8   7.95

WE TOO ARE DRIFTING by Gale Wilhelm. 128 pp. Timeless
Lesbian novel, a masterpiece.   ISBN 0-930044-61-4   6.95

AMATEUR CITY by Katherine V. Forrest. 224 pp. A Kate
Delafield mystery. First in a series.   ISBN 0-930044-55-X   7.95

THE SOPHIE HOROWITZ STORY by Sarah Schulman. 176
pp. Engaging novel of madcap intrigue.   ISBN 0-930044-54-1   7.95

THE BURNTON WIDOWS by Vickie P. McConnell. 272 pp. A
Nyla Wade mystery, second in the series.   ISBN 0-930044-52-5   7.95

OLD DYKE TALES by Lee Lynch. 224 pp. Extraordinary
stories of our diverse Lesbian lives.   ISBN 0-930044-51-7   7.95

DAUGHTERS OF A CORAL DAWN by Katherine V. Forrest.
240 pp. Novel set in a Lesbian new world.   ISBN 0-930044-50-9   7.95

THE PRICE OF SALT by Claire Morgan. 288 pp. A milestone
novel, a beloved classic.   ISBN 0-930044-49-5   8.95

AGAINST THE SEASON by Jane Rule. 224 pp. Luminous,
complex novel of interrelationships.   ISBN 0-930044-48-7   7.95

LOVERS IN THE PRESENT AFTERNOON by Kathleen
Fleming. 288 pp. A novel about recovery and growth.
ISBN 0-930044-46-0   8.95

TOOTHPICK HOUSE by Lee Lynch. 264 pp. Love between
two Lesbians of different classes.   ISBN 0-930044-45-2   7.95

MADAME AURORA by Sarah Aldridge. 256 pp. Historical
novel featuring a charismatic "seer."   ISBN 0-930044-44-4   7.95

CURIOUS WINE by Katherine V. Forrest. 176 pp. Passionate
Lesbian love story, a best-seller.   ISBN 0-930044-43-6   7.95

BLACK LESBIAN IN WHITE AMERICA by Anita Cornwell.
141 pp. Stories, essays, autobiography.   ISBN 0-930044-41-X   7.50

CONTRACT WITH THE WORLD by Jane Rule. 340 pp.
Powerful, panoramic novel of gay life.   ISBN 0-930044-28-2   7.95

YANTRAS OF WOMANLOVE by Tee A. Corinne. 64 pp.
Photos by noted Lesbian photographer.   ISBN 0-930044-30-4   6.95

MRS. PORTER'S LETTER by Vicki P. McConnell. 224 pp.
The first Nyla Wade mystery.   ISBN 0-930044-29-0   7.95

TO THE CLEVELAND STATION by Carol Anne Douglas.
192 pp. Interracial Lesbian love story.   ISBN 0-930044-27-4   6.95

THE NESTING PLACE by Sarah Aldridge. 224 pp. A
three-woman triangle—love conquers all!   ISBN 0-930044-26-6   7.95

THIS IS NOT FOR YOU by Jane Rule. 284 pp. A letter to a
beloved is also an intricate novel.   ISBN 0-930044-25-8   8.95

FAULTLINE by Sheila Ortiz Taylor. 140 pp. Warm, funny,
literate story of a startling family.   ISBN 0-930044-24-X   6.95

THE LESBIAN IN LITERATURE by Barbara Grier. 3d ed.
Foreword by Maida Tilchen. 240 pp. Comprehensive bibliography.
Literary ratings; rare photos.   ISBN 0-930044-23-1   7.95

ANNA'S COUNTRY by Elizabeth Lang. 208 pp. A woman
finds her Lesbian identity.   ISBN 0-930044-19-3   6.95

PRISM by Valerie Taylor. 158 pp. A love affair between two
women in their sixties.   ISBN 0-930044-18-5   6.95

BLACK LESBIANS: AN ANNOTATED BIBLIOGRAPHY
compiled by J. R. Roberts. Foreword by Barbara Smith. 112 pp.
Award-winning bibliography.   ISBN 0-930044-21-5   5.95

THE MARQUISE AND THE NOVICE by Victoria Ramstetter.
108 pp. A Lesbian Gothic novel.   ISBN 0-930044-16-9   4.95

OUTLANDER by Jane Rule. 207 pp. Short stories and essays
by one of our finest writers.   ISBN 0-930044-17-7   6.95

SAPPHISTRY: THE BOOK OF LESBIAN SEXUALITY by
Pat Califia. 2d edition, revised. 195 pp.   ISBN 0-9330044-47-9   7.95

ALL TRUE LOVERS by Sarah Aldridge. 292 pp. Romantic
novel set in the 1930s and 1940s.   ISBN 0-930044-10-X   7.95

A WOMAN APPEARED TO ME by Renee Vivien. 65 pp. A
classic; translated by Jeannette H. Foster.   ISBN 0-930044-06-1   5.00

CYTHEREA'S BREATH by Sarah Aldridge. 240 pp. Romantic
novel about women's entrance into medicine.
    ISBN 0-930044-02-9   6.95

TOTTIE by Sarah Aldridge. 181 pp. Lesbian romance in the
turmoil of the sixties.   ISBN 0-930044-01-0   6.95

THE LATECOMER by Sarah Aldridge. 107 pp. A delicate love
story.   ISBN 0-930044-00-2   5.00